"My name is Scott Ingalls. My men and I represent no government, no business, no cartel, no syndicate. We represent no one but ourselves and our conviction that someone must do something to stem the tide of terrorism. We bring death for dishonor . . . but talk is cheap.

"I am here to tell you what we have just done and issue a warning to the contemptible cowards who slaughter innocent, uninvolved people in the name of warped causes.

"Our job is simple. When terrorists strike and endanger the lives or property of innocents, we will be there. We will strike swiftly, efficiently, and with extreme prejudice. There will never be a trial of a terrorist we attack.

"I instructed our assault team to provide me with evidence of our work."

Ingalls stepped toward the camera and raised his fist. Dangling from his clenched fingers by strands of long dirty black hair, was the severed head of the terrorist leader. The eyes were open and stared blankly; the mouth as agape in a silent scream; and, flies buzzed obscenely around the ragged neck wound.

Scott Ingalls had made his point.

GEOFFREY METCALF

The TERRORIST KILLERS

A Critic's Choice paperback
from Lorevan Publishing, Inc.
New York, New York

ISBN: 1-55547-269-9

First Critic's Choice edition: 1988

From LOREVAN PUBLISHING, INC.

Critic's Choice Paperbacks
31 East 28th Street
New York, New York 10016

Manufactured in the United States of America

To Lindy

Without whose love, support, confidence and consistent "urging" this would still be sequestered in one of the unlabeled boxes I presume to consider files.

Forever and always . . .

This is a work of fiction. If that is good or bad is a subject for debate.

Guerrilla warfare and terrorism are permitted to exist because of the moral and ethical considerations society imposes. The British discovered in Malaysia that the only effective way to combat guerrilla activity was to cordon off areas and deny safe zones for the guerrilla. The same tactic could be used against terrorism except it would require measures civilized societies consider abhorrent. Politics, national pride, and larger-picture-scenarios prevent governments from employing the tactics and strategy this novel presents.

However, one fact remains annoyingly consistent. As long as terrorists have holes to hide in, or rocks to climb under, any effort to eliminate terrorism as a tactic for radical special interest groups is impotent.

The fictional *I.T.* succeeds because of freedom to do so and the resources (money and skill) to act.

There are two cliches which synthesize to create a motto for *I.T.:* Money talks, and bullshit walks; and, The Golden Rule—The Ones with the gold make the rules.

If men with power and money ever link up with men with determination, and tactical martial skills, the potential exists for *I.T.* to become more than a work of fiction, or an exciting evening at the movies.

I.T. could really happen.

—Geoffrey Metcalf

PREFACE

As the large brown and yellow spider crawled across the dirt floor of Scott Ingalls' tent his thoughts were bouncing like ball bearings on a marble floor. He watched the spider with fascination.

He stared into his canteen cup of ice water. His thoughts were of Colonel Jesse Morse making history at this very moment, as Sergeant LaChance was writing another chapter in Greece at the same time. Two of the most significant acts to occur since John F. Kennedy pushed Khrushchev to the limit off Cuba over twenty years ago, or Ronald Reagan ordered the bombing of Tripoli.

This was a long way from The Inn at Castle Hill in Newport, Rhode Island. He was about to put his name in history with two dramatic, some would say renegade, acts of counter-terrorism.

One plan was unfolding in the desert of Libya. A complex plan fraught with split second timing, detailed coordination, and the three elements essential to a successful raid or ambush: surprise; firepower; and, violence of action. The second plan was a last minute "target of opportunity."

The plan was classic and simple.

CHAPTER ONE

The initial celebration was moderate. It consisted of Ingalls and Morse congratulating the troops and passing out the champagne as they continued to pack up for the move out. LaChance and his men joined the celebration and briefed Ingalls and Morse as the tents were folded and loaded onto the waiting aircraft.

". . . and they wanted us to hang around and hold a fucking press conference. Can you believe it?"

"Sergeant, we're real proud of you and your men. The Libyan attack was heavy, but your raid in Athens is the core of what we can expect in the future. You executed it to perfection." Scott smiled.

"Hey, no biggie. The plan was perfect. A troop of Boy Scouts could have done it, sir."

"No, I don't think so friend. It required a group of trained, experienced men who were willing to do what you did."

"Colonel, you should have been there. It was like Vaseline on satin. We were afraid that before the gas got inside, the terrorists might have taken out a few passengers. Shit, they must have been so confused. The stew told us she heard the explosions on the roof and by the time everyone looked up they were dropping like rain. Goddamn, I wish I could have seen that."

"Dictate your briefing into that recorder so Mr. Ingalls can use it when he delivers his press conference," Morse said to the excited LaChance.

Colonel Jesse Morse was a big man: Six feet four inches, 245 pounds. His physical stature matched his reputation as a soldier. He had short cropped white hair, a granitelike square jaw, and, despite his age, muscles that still coiled like a young athlete. He was a living legend and the consumate warrior. Sprague deCamp or Edgar Rice Burroughs would have written volumes about such a hero.

Before the I.T. Operational force departed from the Objective Rallying Point Command Base, Scott walked out to the airstrip to make his announcement to the world. He wore desert camouflage fatigues like everyone else, and a big white cowboy hat Morse had given him. He stood in front of one of the Soviet HOOK helicopters and spoke without notes to the cameraman and two man crew. Mike levels had been preset, reflector panels positioned to light his face. He began.

"My name is Scott Ingalls." Scott was just forty years old, a charismatic enigma. He was just under six feet two inches, and a tad under 200 pounds. His hair was longer than his comrades, and he wore a waxed handlebar moustache. His lady friend once described him as having the style of Fred Astaire and the grace of John Wayne.

"I am the President of an organization called International Terrorist Suppressors. I.T. was founded in an effort to provide a nonpolitical, totally autonomous, freelance anti-terrorist organization. Most reasonable people will acknowledge that terrorism has gotten totally out of hand. It is a tide of dishonorable violence.

"Few people care if foolish petty men choose to kill

each other under the guise of perverted ideologies. However, when such squabbling spills over to touch the lives of innocent men, women and children, it is unconscionable. The problem has been compounded for years by national pride, larger plan concerns, politics and hubris.

"I.T. offers a solution to the problem. We represent no government, no business, no cartel, no syndicate. We represent no one but ourselves and our conviction that *someone* must do something to stem the tide of terrorism. We bring *death for dishonor* . . . and more. Talk is cheap. The last thing we propose to do is add to the quagmire with more rhetoric. I.T. is an action oriented group. We have assembled and trained the very best soldiers in the world.

"I am here to tell you what we have just done, what we will continue to do, and to issue a very serious warning to the contemptible cowards who slaughter innocent, uninvolved people in the name of warped causes.

"Our intelligence sources discovered a terrorist training camp in the Libyan desert which was cousined by Colonel Kadaffi and supported by Russian rubles and equipment. This camp was developing potent chemical and biological agents for use as weapons by terrorist groups. We seized the records from that camp and are now releasing that information to the world press. It includes lists of names of those involved; locations of targets; money and equipment provided and by whom; and, a detailed inventory of the chemical and biological agents that were secured at that site.

"That training facility is no more. It was successfully raided and the occupants terminated. Additionally, we detonated a neutron bomb in the storage facility reducing it to a charged mass of relatively harmless nuclear waste. That is one terrorist coin which will not be spent. Our coin is *violence of action*, and a solution to terrorism.

"We did this as a message to terrorists everywhere. While we were conducting this exercise, we heard of the Pan Am hijacking in Athens. One hour after we received that report, and with our forces en route to Lybia, we dispatched another team to Athens.

"By now, you know the results of that effort. We were able to do that because we report to no government, no committees. Our job is simple. When terrorists strike and endanger the lives or property of innocents, we will be there. We will strike swiftly, efficiently, and with extreme prejudice. There will never be a trial of a terrorist we attack.

"In Athens we terminated ten terrorists. They were each shot once in the head with a 240 grain bullet fired from a 44 magnum pistol. The leader of that terrorist squad was not shot. In order to provide proof that we are the group conducting this crusade, and as a deterrent to future terrorists, I instructed the assault team to provide me with evidence of our work." Scott lifted up the head of the terrorist leader and held it in front of the camera. It hung from his fist by long dirty black hair. The eyes were open and stared blankly; and mouth was agape in a silent scream; flys buzzed obscenely around the ragged neck wound. He held it before the camera for six seconds, then threw it into the sand.

"Extreme evil requires extreme justice. I am here to tell you that no terrorist anywhere in the world is safe from us. We will find you wherever you hide. Anyone who aides terrorists shall be treated as a terrorist. Any fool who commits an act of terrorism from this moment forward will be signing the death warrant of his parents, wife, and children. Towns that harbor terrorists will have their police chiefs and mayors assassinated and court houses destroyed.

Henceforth, terrorism is forbidden by order of International Terrorists Suppressors."

"That's a take boss."

"Okay Jim, make dups for NBC, CBS, ABC, BBC, and CNN. Have a transcript printed and send that also. Be sure copies of the transcript go to Reuters, AP and UPI, all the newspapers, *Pravda,* Tass and anyone else you can think of."

"You got it, Mr. Ingalls. You're about to become one very famous man."

"Yeah, wanted by every police department, security agency and terrorist in the world. I can hardly wait."

"Lighten up, sport," grinned Morse. "We're gonna take better care of you than the crown jewels."

"Colonel, why is that only moderately reassuring."

"Come on, Scotty. When we get to France, Ben Slade will probably want to kiss you."

"Well, if you can't keep me alive, please don't let Ben kiss me."

"I think Miss Leslie will see to that, pal."

And on that parting note they departed Egypt for the trip to the south of France.

CHAPTER TWO

Senator Calvin Pastor and his wife Jennifer walked over the little bridge at Chappaquiddick. They were Madison Avenue's concept of what a political couple should be. Handsome, pretty, and clean-cut; family oriented; superb backgrounds; strong, consistent ideals; respected by both allies and opponents; intelligent, decisive, and, right now, more than a little tired and frustrated.

"Poor Ted," said Calvin.

"Ted who?" asked Jennifer.

"Kennedy. The poor dumb son of a bitch."

"Hey, you play—you pay."

"Yeah, I guess."

"Are you still down about Scott?"

"What's to be down. He's been passing out money like rock stars. I hate to admit it, but it's been six months since there have been any hijackings or kidnappings, or bombings or *any* '-ings' to do with terrorism. I guess he really *did* scare some people."

"No one has heard from him, have they?"

"No one is sure. According to some of the guys in Intelligence, there have been some conversations with his representatives about cooperation in the future. Strictly sub rosa, you understand."

"Hey, I have an idea. Let's get someone to stay with Steven tonight, and you and I go off-island for dinner."

"You got a date, lady. And I know just the place. Scott took me there after midterms one year a century ago."

"Where?"

"To the oldest continually operating tavern in the country."

"Not in Philadelphia?"

"Nope. Just about thirty miles from here in Newport, Rhode Island. The White Horse Tavern. You hit the shower first. I'll call for reservations."

Two hours later, Senator and Mrs. Pastor walked up the brick walk and into The White Horse Tavern.

"Reservations for two, Pastor," Calvin said.

"Certainly, Senator. They're just setting your table now. Would you like to wait in the bar? There's a table by the fire."

"Thank you."

They went into the small bar where George Washington, Benedict Arnold, John Adams, et al had once been served libations. As they sat down the bartender marched over to the table and deposited two drinks.

"A Jack Daniels and water for the lady; a Laphroig on the rocks for the good Senator."

Calvin looked at Jennifer, and they both smiled.

"That's more than a good guess, barkeep," said Calvin.

"They've been paid for already, Senator." The bartender said and walked back behind the bar.

"Someone must have recognized us," said Jennifer.

"Apparently someone who knows us pretty well. How could they have given him the order without us seeing?" Calvin asked.

"Well, we had reservations. Maybe someone you know noticed."

"Whatever. A free drink is a free drink. Cheers."

"Do you know how rare it is for a bar to even *have* Laphroig?" he said to his wife. They were interrupted by the host.

"Your table is ready, Senator. Right this way. Please be careful ma'am, the stairs are rather narrow and quite steep." They walked up the staircase to the second floor.

The small upstairs dining room was empty except for one table set for three. As the host seated them Calvin turned to say, "There must be some mistake, there will only be two for dinner."

"Yes, sir. I'll send someone to take care of the other setting." The host walked away suppressing a thin grin.

"Have we just walked into the twilight zone?" asked Jennifer.

"No, just a small reunion," announced Scott as he approached the table.

"*Scott!*" shouted Calvin. "Are you crazy? In a public restaurant? Christ, we're just a half mile from the Navy War College. Are you *asking* to be caught?"

"Excitable isn't he, Jen?" Scott said as he leaned over to kiss her cheek.

"Scott, this *must* be dangerous. How did you know we would be here?" she asked.

"The drinks. I should have known. The drinks. There can't be a hundred people in Rhode Island that've ever even heard of Laphroig, let alone know I crave it," mumbled Calvin.

"Let's sit down, have a nice dinner and chat." Scott smiled.

"Why are you taking this risk? Do you want to be caught?" rasped the Senator.

"No, not at all. If you'll just sit and calm down I'll explain."

Calvin sat down opposite his wife. Scott moved to sit between them with his back to the wall.

"I always liked this place. Has great clam chowder even if they do use too much dill."

"Scott!"

"Okay, okay. No more games. I'm in Newport to talk to an elite group of students at the Navy War College. Yeah, the administration *is* kinda sorta cooperating with us so long as no one admits it. Willy Bond was in here when your reservation came in. So he called, and I made some arrangements. Everyone in the tavern at this moment, except for the host, is under my command. We effectively have the place to ourselves for the evening."

"Why?" asked Calvin.

"So we wouldn't be disturbed, of course." Scott smiled as he extracted a short cigar from a leather case taken from his inside jacket pocket.

"No, I mean why have you risked meeting?"

"Oh. Well, when we last spoke I told you if I survived that last hit on me we would talk, and I would answer your question about 'Why I.T.'?"

"I must confess, I never expected to see you again. Are you sure you're safe here?"

"I couldn't be safer. There is a perimeter so tight around this building right now the cops in the police station across the street will have a hard time getting to their cars."

"You are certainly something else," commented Jennifer.

"I've been called much worse. By the way, if you don't mind, I took the liberty of ordering dinner for us so we wouldn't have to be interrupted with menus and such."

"Not at all. So, why? No. Hold that. Before 'Why' tell me 'How?' " asked the Senator as he sipped his ten year old unblended scotch.

CHAPTER THREE

As soon as he had heard the newscast, Senator Pastor called Scott's office only to find he had sold the agency and wasn't expected back. He then called Scott's private number at his home on Commonwealth Avenue in Boston to learn that the condo had been sold also, and no, Mr. Ingalls hadn't left a forwarding address. Next he buzzed his chief of staff and while he was waiting for him to come in, he again picked up the phone and called his wife.

"Jen, have you heard about Scott?"

"Who hasn't? Cal, can this be real?"

"Honey, I'm afraid it's all *too* real. What's more, he told me about the idea when we went fishing, but he said it was a concept for some client's movie. I should have known something wasn't right. I just hope we don't get involved. It's the last thing I need right now. Especially with the tax proposal coming up for debate. I can't afford to be tainted in anyway. That son of a bitch. He used me! God, he played me like a violin, just like we were back in school. If anybody calls, we haven't seen him and don't know anything about where he is."

"Well, it's true we don't know where he is, but I

already told that Mr. Ivers that he visited a few months ago and that you two went fishing."

"Oh shit! Ivers is with the FBI."

"Cal, I couldn't see the harm in telling the truth. We haven't seen him since then."

"Don't fret babe. You couldn't have known. Look, go to the club and play a round of golf. Play slow. I'll meet you there for dinner. And for Christssake don't talk to *anybody* about our terrorist friend."

"Cal, what does this mean?"

"It means you are going to play golf for an afternoon. A full eighteen holes."

"I'll see you at the club."

When he hung up the telephone, his chief of staff, Thorton Morris, another college friend of Pastor's, entered the office. Calvin's age, Morris was growing toward fat. His dirty blonde hair was both thinning and graying, and his suit, although expensive, didn't look it.

"Hey, did you hear about Ingalls?"

"The whole fucking world has heard, about Ingalls. That's why you're in here Thorton. Sit down, and be brilliant."

The freshman Senator, prodigal son of the former Speaker of the House, and one time friend of Scott Ingalls proceeded to tell his chief of staff about his fishing trip with Ingalls three months earlier, in exact detail.

"Well, that's it. Or perhaps I should say that's I.T. How bad can I get hurt?"

"Jesus, Senator, the timing sucks."

"Don't belabor the obvious, Thorton. Advise me! Where do we go from here?"

"Well, the bright side is you didn't give him any money. Did you?"

"No, I didn't give him any money. But I did tell him how to grease the right wheels. I did offer a complete analysis of the situation. I did tell him he was out of his fucking mind, and would probably be indicted by everyone with a pen and marked for assassination by everyone with a gun." Calvin fished in his jacket pocket for his pipe and pouch and began stuffing tobacco into the bowl.

"We only have one route really, and we need to move quick. Employ a tried and true business technique. Pass the buck. Accuse Ingalls of misusing your trust, say he was talking about a movie script for a client, and then hide and hope for the best."

"What if he actually *does* something. You know, kill Arafat, or blow up an IRA headquarters or something."

"Well, legally you know as well as I do, you can't be tagged as an accessory. You had no prior knowledge."

"That's the exact phrase I *don't* want my opponents using. I'm the bright fair-haired lad. I'm not supposed to be duped by con men and charlatans. I'm supposed to be able to see through all that bullshit and attack the essence of situations."

"Cal, lighten up, will you? Sure, it's bad you met with the guy, but it isn't *that* bad."

"Is that like the difference between being pregnant and 'a little pregnant'?"

"Look, so he used your friendship to gain insight and maybe refine his plan. You categorically refused to get involved when you thought he was serious, and then he backed off and lied. In addition to that, a whole herd of heavyweight tycoons were taken for a lot more than your shattered friendship. I mean, this guy got in the pants of almost every big business in this country, and apparently in a few overseas too. At least you're in good company in your misery."

"I don't find that consoling. Okay, draft a statement for the press, and make a list of who I should call in State, the Bureau, CIA, Treasury, and whoever else you can think of. Meanwhile, I have to prepare for this tax issue debate. Scott, why couldn't you have stayed out of my life? Oh yeah, and get me Ivers at the Bureau. He's already talked to Jennifer, and I want to call him before he calls me."

CHAPTER FOUR

Jennifer put down her wine glass and stared at Scott. "Scott, I'm supposed to be a sophisticated woman. I've had a privileged life: the best schools, the best clothes, social opportunity. I may not be as comfortable with risk taking as Leslie. She always had equal parts of brass and class. But I *still* find all this a bit overwhelming."

"Goddamn crazy would be closer to the mark," said Calvin.

"Overwhelming. Crazy. Both are relative. To me anyone seeking public office in today's political environment is crazy," said Scott.

"Scott, before your Colonel Morse and before the money men, how did your 'I.T.' ever actually start?" asked Jennifer.

"Yeah? Where did it all begin?" asked Calvin.

"Ah, well, I guess you could say 'Once upon a time,' " started Scott.

August in Newport, Rhode Island is a sea breeze and sun anachronism of times gone by. Scott Ingalls sat on the long sloping lawn in front of the Inn at Castle Hill and watched the tide take out the sail boats between Jamestown and Newport and felt a disquieting jaded frustration. He was sitting on a heavy cedar beach chair with his feet up on a white wrought iron table. He appeared sufficiently Newport-casual in Izod and Topsiders with a cotton sweater draped over his shoulders. He put down his Becks dark beer to bite the end off his Dunhill Monte Cruz cigar. Yet as the cooling southwesterly wind mellowed the afternoon sun, and the yuppie groupies played backgammon and sipped mimosas, he felt useless and wrong.

"Why do you do that?" asked the woman plopping down next to him in the sister cedar chair.

"Do what?" he asked.

"Why do you bite the end off those disgusting ropes when I paid fifty bucks for that fancy gold cigar cutter of yours?" She was thirty-one years old, five feet eight inches tall, about 130 pounds. Her name was Leslie Campbell. She was third generation rich, an homogeneous product of Pembroke, Smith, Vassar and a year in Europe (for the 'experience').

"Sorry, I forget I have it sometimes, and I'm used to biting the end off." As he said this he picked pieces of tobacco off his tongue.

"Well, you're not in the Army anymore, and although it might be terribly macho, it's also gross." She rubbed sun shield on her already freckled nose.

"Man is a product of both experience and environment love." He took a swig of beer from the bottle.

"Scott, there are times . . ."

". . . time for you and time for me, and time yet for a hundred decisions and revisions which a moment will erase." He killed the beer with a deep long pull.

"T.S. Eliot, the Lovesong of J. Alfred what's his name."

"Prufrock."

"Yeah, Prufrock. Don't do that to me!" she scowled as he laughed.

"Scott, you are a pain in the tush sometimes. You

bounce back and forth between Ying and Yang faster than a Chinese ping pong match. You're so damn frustrating. You have almost everything to make you wonderful: looks, brains, money, charisma . . ."

". . . a gold Rolex watch and a partridge in a pear tree," he finished singing the Samilian melody.

"Why do you have to be such a butt? You know, people might admire you or even respect you, but people don't really *like* you."

"Les, I know all that, but I'm really not in the mood for one of your lectures. Look, people admire me because I look and sound good and have the right ribbons. People respect me for what I have done and what I can do for them. And people don't like me for precisely the same reasons, and because I am an enigma, and enigmas cause confusion, frustration and dislike." He rose up out of his chair and pulled his sweater over his head.

"Now, where are you going?" She threw down her sun lotion.

"First, I'm going to visit *la salle de bains;* then I'm going to grab my scuba gear, and try to spear a thirty pound striper. Failing that, I'll settle for a few tautog so we don't have to eat out again tonight. I'll see you at the cottage in a few hours. Put the roof down on the car like a good girl, and we can drive along Ocean Drive on our way into town to pick up some wine."

As he pulled on his wet suit, Scott was thinking about what was on the news. The TWA hijacking dominated the front page and six and eleven o'clock news. The whole concept of terrorism frustrated him and genuinely pissed him off. It wasn't so much the actual acts of bombings, kidnapping and murder. He had participated in far worse as an A-team commander in both his tours in Vietnam. Back then, they would kidnap some village chief, interrogate him, murder him (although they called it 'assassination'), and then make it look like Charlie had done it. But that was different.

Regardless of what they did or did not call it, it was War. There were sides drawn—the good guys and the bad guys—black and white (although the numerous shades of gray often got in the way). Despite the chaos, there was some order.

Terrorism, when it's spread into the common everyday lives of civilians, was flat ass wrong. And the most awful part was the arbitrary and capricious manner in which it was practiced.

Scott permitted himself to wallow in his convoluted logic for a time, then reminded himself of rule Number One: 'No one ever said it was going to be fair.' Still, he couldn't help but come back to the point that someone ought to do *something*.

He descended to about sixty feet in the blue-green water and started to swim toward the ledge off Castle Hill. The cool quiet of the ocean and the current helped to crystalize his thoughts. The focus of his frustration and anger wasn't any altruistic good versus evil conflict. The real core of his feelings was the lack of control. And, more specifically, that *he* couldn't exercise any control in the matter.

Just then a large silver blur cut in front of him. It was a small school of squid. He raised his spear gun as what was chasing them came speeding out of the dark and into his field of vision. It was a good size striped bass. No, three of them. He aimed at the second fish and fired, hitting it just behind the gills. It hung in the water at the end of his spear line for a moment. Then it erupted in a burst of energy, and tried to swim away towing him a few feet until he hauled it close enough to get hold of it.

As he started his 600 yard swim back to shore with dinner, he wondered if only one could capture and control events as easily as that bass.

"Here's dinner," he said putting the thirty-four pound fish in the sink so that both head and tail sprouted from each side.

"Wow. Nice fish. That'll feed us for weeks. However, you caught it—you clean it. Then I'll cook it."

"Okay, but after I clean it, let's take that drive into town. I want to bounce an idea off your hard head." He proceeded to scale and filet the large fish.

"You mean the Bastard of Boylston Street wants my little ole opinion about something other than what tie goes with what jacket?"

"As a matter of fact I want your opinion on my concept for making the world a better place to live."

"Kind of heavy for a sundown ride along Ocean Drive isn't it, hon?" She lighted a cigarette from the gas stove.

"How about discussing my idea for a series of television commercials for your computer client using the more bizarre elements of the Kama Sutra as metaphor?"

"No, I was thinking more of an international, nonpolitical anti-terrorism organization funded by world business." He threw the carcass into a plastic garbage bag.

"Hey that wouldn't be a bad TV series: 'Son of A-Team Meets Mission Impossible'."

"Actually Les, that's kind of what I have in mind, but not for television. For real." He continued washing his hands and squeezing lemon juice into his palms.

"Are you nuts?"

"That, my love, is what they said about Wilson when he proposed the League of Nations, and about NATO, NASA, and Ted Turner. No sweet cheeks, I am flat ass serious. And moreover, I believe that properly structured, promoted, and managed, it can work."

"And I think you've got a nitrogen bubble in your brain. Do you want to go to the hospital? Tell you what, fella, the top's down on the Morgan. Let's go for that ride and you can tell me all about the kind of dreams opium produces."

They walked out of the cottage and got into Scott's yellow Morgan and sped off toward Bailey's Beach where Eisenhower, Kennedy and the boys used to get their Presidential sunburns.

"Leslie, this isn't as nuts as you might think."

To their right was the Atlantic Ocean with the sound of fog horns in the background, and seagulls eavesdropping.

"Okay, blue eyes, talk. I'll smell the low tide."

Scott divided his attention between shifting the Morgan through the numerous turns in the road and his monologue.

"All right, here's the concept. Hold the sarcasm until I'm done, okay?"

She smiled and flipped her hair in the wind.

"Everyone acknowledges that this whole international terrorism thing is totally out of line. It's far worse than the old Kingston Trio song about 'the French hate the Germans, the Germans hate the Poles, Italians hate Yugoslavs,' and so on. Between the Red Brigade, Khadaffi, the IRA, the Shiites, and all the others fringe fanatics, it is becoming a virtual crap shoot when you travel internationally. The problem is compounded by all the political crap that invariably gets in the way. Terrorism is directed at countries, but it attacks individuals—usually innocent individuals. If these were your normal criminals the cops would go in, do their number, and that would be it. But these aren't normal criminals and everyone knows that. If terrorists attack

America by hijacking an airliner with some American citizens on board and end up in say Lebanon, America can't act directly. It becomes an international political football. Although some poor grandmother from Bismarck, North Dakota is the victim, the goddamn State Department has to deal with it like some Russian diplomat got nailed for drunk driving after an embassy party in D.C.

"When I was teaching at Fort Benning we used to teach there are three elements essential to a successful ambush: surprise; firepower; and, violence of action. Terrorists know this, and use those elements. However, the governments of the world are hamstrung to respond in kind. The reason is inherent—they are *governments*, answerable to a myriad of individuals and policies, and larger plan scenarios."

Scott downshifted to negotiate a turn at the top of a hill. "So, you have a 'Catch 22,' " Leslie interrupted, "which has no good solution. You have to have those rules, even if they stink. Otherwise the Israelis would be killing Arabs on Rodeo Drive, and Gucci would never stand for that any more than the Beverly Hills Chamber of Commerce would."

"That's the whole point, there need to be rules. But there also has to be some omniscient benevolent *something* that is above the rules. Some avenging archangel who can deal with terrorism *with* terrorism. Death *for* Dishonor. Without having to wade through the inevitable cesspool of bureaucratic politics."

"Okay, Ingalls, cut through the rhetoric, and spit out your grand solution."

"What I propose, Les, is an organization comprised of those who have the most to lose from unchecked international terrorism." He took out another cigar, started to bite the end off, stopped, reached in his jacket for the gold cigar cutter, clipped the end off, and lighted it.

"So you're going to organize grandmothers from Bismarck to attack terrorism?" She grinned.

"No, babe, I'm talking about big business. The *Fortune 500* and their international counterparts, like Triad and the Cartels. We organize a Board of Directors made up of all the heavyweight CEO's we can get and they fund the project. In turn, they appoint an Executive Committee comprised of one member from each region of the world to address operational needs. The Executive Committee in turn tasks the Operational Forces with missions to attack terrorists both in reaction to acts of terrorism and in preemptive strikes against anticipated threats. Or in your words, 'The A-Team meets Mission Impossible.' "

"You're crazy! It would never work. Besides, do you think for a moment that the various governments are going to sanction some half-assed freelance army traipsing around the world fighting for truth, justice, and the capitalist ideal?"

"First, yes. I may be crazy, but I'm crazy with revulsion over what is permitted to go on because of "technicalities." Second, it will work. And third, screw the governments. Who do you think really controls government anyway? Not the President, not legislative bodies, and certainly not the general constituents. Governments are controlled by business. And if the world-wide brotherhood of the bottom line say 'turn your back Uncle, we'll handle this,' I say it can work."

"I think you stand a snowball's chance in hell of ever seeing any of this even coming close to happening. However, I know you well enough to know that you are going to take a shot. So what do you have in mind?"

"Les, it's not as crazy as it may seem. Ross Perot from EDS did it when some of his executives were snatched in

Iran. Bull Simmons led the raid. I knew Bull when I was at Benning. We talked after he pulled the Son Tay raid in North Vietnam."

"Scott, that was Vietnam, and Perot got lucky. Besides Simmons is dead."

"There are other Bull Simmons, and Perot didn't just get lucky. He had a good plan with good people, good training, and sound leadership. Look. When Mussolini was captured, the Germans got him out in a daring raid led by Skorzini which everyone said was impossible. The Israelis went right into Kampala and pulled out a whole plane full of people right under Idi Amin's big nose. It is *not* ridiculous."

"And just how the hell do you intend to get the *Fortune 500* and their cousins to cooperate with you in this venture?"

"I'm going to sell it to them. Just like selling pens: there is a need; we have something to fulfill that need; you overcome the objections; identify any hidden objections; and, you close."

"You're going to sell it—just like a Bic pen?"

"More like a Mont Blanc Diplomat."

They pulled into a small shopping center on Bellvue Avenue across from the Tennis Hall of Fame. Scott switched off the motor and turned to look at Leslie.

"I suppose if anyone can sell this scatterbrained prime time series you have a better shot than most. But don't be surprised if you end up on the FBI's 'most disturbed' list. Now go get the wine, and I'll bake you the catch of the day."

CHAPTER FIVE

Jennifer was playing with her food as her husband looked at Scott with a blank stare.

"Scott, the one thing you never told me is how you put the pieces together. Oh, you said plenty about motive, and need, and dedication. But you never told me how you put the financial base together, or where you found the men for your own private little army. I've seen your Colonel Morse and except for some allusions to time you spent in Nam together, I'm not clear on how you got him or any of the others."

"I asked," said Scott.

"Come on. What did you do? Pick up the phone and say 'Hey, Colonel. I served with you over a decade ago, and I want you to help me kill bad guys?' "

"Not exactly. But you're not far off the mark. Of course, I didn't telephone. I went to see him in person.

Colonel Jesse Morse sat at the corner table in the cocktail lounge of the Fort Benning Officers Club sipping his Jack Daniels. Morse was a big man, above average, and although he was forty-eight years old, he was still in great shape. He was both imposing and sad. The consummate warrior without any more wars to fight, and a career about to end. He had five rows of ribbons scattered among which were a Distinguished Service Cross, three Silver Stars, five Bronze Stars, three Purple Hearts. The sum was the result of thirty years in the Army. He also had collected a Combat Infantryman's Badge with Star; Ranger tab; Master Parachutist badge; Pathfinder badge; Skin-diver badge; Jungle Warfare patch; and, was authorized to wear any one of five foreign sets of jump-wings. However, he normally wore only his class A uniform with CIB, jump-wings and Ranger tab. He didn't need to advertise, any one who mattered knew. Jesse Morse was a goddamn living legend.

He had been surprised to hear from Scott Ingalls. They hadn't seen each other since Fort Bragg ten years earlier when Morse tried (unsuccessfully) to talk Scott into staying in the Army. It was too bad. Ingalls was good. Hell, any kid that led an A-team for two tours was good. But Ingalls was special. He was as strong and as smart as most of his troopers, and could have been the model for FM 22-100 on leadership. But the thing that really distinguished him was something that would never show up on an OER (Officer Evaluation Report)—he was, without question, the luckiest man Morse had ever met. He earned his only Purple Heart in a hand-to-hand fight with a Viet Cong guerrilla. He wasn't wounded by the VC. While they were wrestling on the ground, Scott rolled over some barb wire which cut his butt. Morse wrote him up for a Purple Heart figuring the kid was too lucky to ever get a righteous wound.

Scott entered the lounge from the pool side door and had to wait for a moment to let his eyes adjust to the semi-dark. He was squeezing his eyes shut and counting to himself when he heard the familiar voice.

"Ingalls, get your butt over here—now!"

Snapping to attention—old habits die hard—he spotted Morse in the corner and jogged over while the others in the bar stared at the long-haired civilian with a handlebar moustache double-timing to Colonel Morse's table.

"Sir. Major Ingalls, Scott C. reporting as ordered, sir." He snapped a salute.

"Who the hell made you a Major?" asked Morse.

"The Army Reserve, sir," he answered still at attention.

"Well that figures." Breaking the ice, he stood up and shook hands with Scott.

"Good to see you sport. Have a seat."

"Good to see you too, sir." He sat down and motioned for the waitress to come over.

"Gee, for an old man you look like you're still in fair shape, Colonel."

"Scotty me lad, I may be a bit long of tooth, but I can still march twenty-five miles, drink a bottle of J.D., and kick your young butt."

"I don't doubt it boss," he said as the waitress arrived.

"Chivas rocks, double, for me. And Jack Daniels double for my father here." Scott smiled to the waitress.

"So, what brings you to Fort Benning? If it's for a haircut and a shave, I'll do it for you myself."

"Colonel, I flew down from Boston just to see you." He took out a leather cigar case and pulled out two Dunhill panatellas, handing one to Morse.

"Life must be good if you can afford these." The colonel bit the end off his cigar and struck a match.

"Business has been good—the verdict is still out on life." He mimicked the cigar routine.

"You flew 1200 miles for a counseling session son?"

"No sir. I flew 1200 miles to get the opinion of a man I respect about a concept which may be either the most innovative and daring venture of our time; or, the most absurd idea since women in Jump School. But we can get into that over dinner. What does the Department of the Army have a living legend do to earn his keep besides serve as a role model for the Queen of Battle?''

''I'm a short timer, son. This is my last tour. I'm serving as head of the Ranger department for five more months. Then I'm gonna do some Elk hunting in Colorado, Trout fishing in Alaska, and probably make a lousy civilian. Oh, I've got a couple of offers from law enforcement agencies, and Brad Hooper offered me a gig working for The Company, but I don't know yet. Shit, if Hooper can be a GS-15, I'm not so sure I'd fit in.''

''Colonel, I've got a private plane parked over at Larson Field. Let's get you in some mufti and I'll fly us to Atlanta for a dinner I promise you won't soon forget.''

''Son, you got yourself a deal, and the tab.'' As the two most significant men in future history rose to leave, they were again stared at by the confused young officers entering the lounge.

During the plane ride to Atlanta, Scott outlined the concept of his terrorist solution. Morse listened intently, occasionally asking a question or making a pertinent comment. As they were awaiting landing instructions from the tower in Atlanta the Colonel said, ''Son, the idea isn't all that totally bad. Your points about Kampala and Skorzini are well taken, and I especially like the Perot example, but you've got one monumental hurdle none of those others had.''

''And that is?'' asked Scott.

''Politics, sport. Sure, tactically we both know those kinds of missions can be duplicated. But with the Perot EDS mission, you had one company with a vested interest—

their people—which had the power, control and money to package the job; and one man with the brass, Perot, to make the committment. You'll never get that kind of singleness of purpose from a goddamn committee of multinationals."

"Colonel, the singleness of purpose is greed. Terrorism impacts on the ability of business to do business. What is good for business is good for the Board, and what is bad for business is bad for the Board. That is the singleness of purpose needed."

"I don't know, Scotty, I think you're talking about an absolute FUBAR political can of worms."

"Colonel, let me ask you a direct and important question. *If* I can put this together—the Board, the funding, the mission requests—would you command the operational task force?" He had started his glide into the airport.

"Ingalls, *if* you can solve the myriad political problems, and actually get world-wide business to support this concept, there is no way in heaven that you could keep me out. Besides which, if you can pull this off—and mind you, I think you'll need more than even your ration of luck to make it fly—you're going to need a living legend with thirty years experience and brass to match yours. You couldn't keep me away."

"Airborne!" shouted Scott.

"All the way, son—and then some by the looks of it."

At dinner that night it was agreed they had a viable concept; and, the military leader for the operational task force. Now all Ingalls had to do was convince four or five hundred companies throughout the world that it was in their collective best interest to fund and support the concept.

Scott outlined a marketing plan for contacting the CEO's and selling them the concept. He was going to start by organizing a steering committee of thirty executives who would help with the networking effort and add clout to the initial pitch. Scott would confide the concept to one U.S. Senator, an old college friend, and have him feel out the potential stumbling blocks anticipated with the State Department and the CIA.

It was agreed that within six months they would hold a seminar in Geneva, Switzerland to pitch the concept and solicit support. Colonel Morse agreed to conduct the recruiting effort to fill the key staff positions needed for the headquarters detachment, keeping in mind that it would be necessary to recruit from various countries so that the flavor of the task force would indeed be international. Morse also came up with a name over his ninth Jack Daniels—I.T.: International Terrorist Suppressors. Since it had to be international, and their prime mission was to suppress terrorists, it made sense, and it sounded good.

CHAPTER SIX

"Leslie, I want you to take the *Fortune 500* and divide them into thirty groups. Take the top thirty and list them first. Then take the bottom thirty and bounce back and forth from top to bottom so that there is a relatively even mix of the mega-large and the just plain large on each list. Then take this second list of international companies and do a separate breakdown. We'll meet with the steering committee for a networking session to determine who knows who. Wherever possible we want to approach a company from a peer level first so that we can presell this thing prior to Geneva. Switzerland will be the stage for the formal charter, but I want this all presold prior to leaving." He sat down at his computer to compose the first draft of the letter he would send to the steering committee members.

Dear__________:

I am writing you on a recommendation from _, of the__________company, concerning an issue of great import to all of us.

I represent a group of businessmen who recognize that anything which negatively impacts on our ability to do business needs to be addressed, and addressed in strong terms from a unified position of strength. Whether it is confiscatory tax practices, arbitrary tariffs, or governmental intervention into business, it needs to be corrected.

One of the more contemptible and far reaching elements of our contemporary world, which impacts on our ability to do business, is the effect of world-wide terrorism.

When a plane is hijacked, it hurts more than just the airline industry, or tourism. The ripple effect of such atrocities eventually is felt on the bottom line of numerous businesses which are not directly involved.

Terrorism in Jamaica hurts airlines and local tourism, but it also effects the bauxite market; which effects the aluminum market; which effects the beer and soft drink-market; and, the retail markets, as well as the trucking industry and so on down the line.

Several of your counterparts, throughout the international business world, are joining forces to address methods for combating the negative business results of world-wide terrorism.

Your participation in the formation of a group of international businesses to examine and report on available alternatives for the problems created by terrorism is invited. It has been suggested, by Mr.__________, that you would be a great asset to such a group; and, that you personally could lend a great deal of input to us during the initial stages of our research and organizational development.

I will call you the week of__________in an effort to establish a mutually convenient time for you and I to meet to discuss our plans in greater detail and to solicit your input and support. I look forward to meeting you and explaining in greater detail what we are considering.It is bold and innovative. It is potentially very good for your business, and certainly good for international business in general.

Please feel free to contact Mr.__________ as a reference for my background, credentials and seriousness.

Most sincerely,

Scott C. Ingalls
President/Chief Executive Officer

''Well, what do you think, Les?'' asked Scott.

''As usual, it's a good letter. But it doesn't say anything specific,'' she answered.

''Precisely! I don't want to outline the concept in writing—yet. What the letter does do, and say, is appeal to the CEO's ego by implying that he is important enough to join this group of his peers with some grand purpose.

''It further suggests he is important to the formation of the group. It uses a reference he knows and can talk to personally. It implies that what we propose will be good for his business. And that he will be part of some elite group with world-wide out reach.''

''Honey, these guys are such big time, do you really think you stand a shot by appealing to their egos?''

''Babe, the two key elements of the contact letter are ego and profit. When you deal at this level, ego and profit are their bloody religion. To try for a 'greater good' or some altruistic crap would be futile. Ego and profit are the keys.'' He reread the letter again to himself.

"And another thing, Les. None of these honchos are going to receive the letter blind. Before they get it, I intend to have the man referenced contact them first to inform them they will be receiving the letter, telling them they should consider it seriously, and definitely meet with me. The networking and positioning are more important than the content of the letter. The letter isn't intended to sell them on anything. It is just an excuse for me to call, and a reason for them to talk to me. By leaving out the most pertinent elements of the concept they need to meet with me to hear what I have to say, and what their colleague has said is important for them to hear."

"Well, blue eyes, you're the marketing whiz. I suppose time will tell, huh?"

CHAPTER SEVEN

Scott Ingalls and Colonel Jesse Morse sat in a corner booth in the pub room of the Lenox Hotel on Boylston Street in Boston eating roast beef sandwiches and drinking beer.

"Okay, son, what've you got?" asked Morse.

"Intelligence reports have identified the location of a terrorist training camp in Libya, funded and run by Khadaffi and friends. It occupies about 460 acres of nothing with the compound dominating a little less than 100 acres. Very Spartan. It consists of administrative buildings, a supply building and a warehouse; indoor ranges; and, the full spectrum of outdoor ranges for everything from pistols to 82mm mortars. They have obstacle courses adjacent to the PT area, and here's the gem—a building full of computer equipment for training in computer sabotage."

"How many troops, and what kind of physical security measures?" asked Morse between bites of his sandwich.

"Cadre consists of a normal battalion size organization of about fifteen officer types, and a homogeneous collection of instructors who reportedly are mostly Arabs with a sprinkling of Russians, the latter no doubt watching their investment. A total cadre of 106. Additionally, there are normally about 200 'students/trainees' at a time."

"Training program?"

"Primarily direct action stuff; raids, ambushes. Ranger kind of missions. But they are also diversified for the 'Advanced' students: kidnapping, assassination squads, computer games, and—this I don't like—biological warfare."

"Are you sure about that, Scotty?" Morse put down his sandwich.

"Afraid so. Both on site agents reported the same information three days apart. Worse still, we heard from both the South Africans and the KGB that the recent Anthrax outbreak in the Sudan was a 'field experiment.' "

"So, is it fair to assume that this is our first hard target?"

"Colonel, it is important that you and I understand one another better than anyone else in the world. The Board has appointed the Executive Committee, and the Executive Committee is, as we speak, going through the motions of approving this first suggested I.T. mission to attack the plague of international terrorism. Colonel, that is the form—we are the substance. When you get back to your office in New York, you will find a Warning Order from me encrypted on your terminal. I took the liberty of drafting the Frag Order for you to zip off to your staff and unit leaders. Bullerwell is already on the Concorde and will probably get to New York about the same time as you. Kapstein is collecting favors in the form of satellite photos of the camp and the Sudan site. Xing and Rucker are setting up the Operational Training Base in West Texas, and Willy Bond has gone shopping."

"Scott, am I to assume it doesn't matter what the Committee decides? That you intend to have us go ahead with or without Board approval?"

"Colonel, the Board and the Committee are important

elements of I.T., but they are only important insofar as they provide the form and the means for us to do the job we all agree is important. The committee could spend two weeks discussing this mission; its import; and, the potential world-wide reaction to what we're doing. You and I know in two weeks we can have that camp reduced to a dark smudge on the desert floor. We will not be hobbled by politics and rhetoric. It is important that we keep the Board and the committee involved in the development and operations of I.T. But don't get confused and start to think of them as the Department of the Army or the State Department, because they are not. They are kind of like a big Chamber of Commerce. A bunch of busy executives who take time out from their important full time jobs to devote some part-time effort to a club which is supposed to help business. In reality, what they seek in the organization is the elitism, and camaraderie of the group, and the ego strokes of the bigger and better and more special. They may feel they are using us to better position themselves for the purposes of business and influence. We, in turn, are using them as a means to an end. We are all rather symbiotic whores. The differences are basic: the executives are in this for power, positioning, profit and ego; you and I may get those things, but our primary mission is to kick ass and take names.'' Scott had both his hands on the table in front of him and he was looking directly into Morse's eyes.

''Scotty, I have always thought highly of you. You were a good leader and a good soldier. However, I never realized the awesome potential you camouflaged. You are one devious, dedicated sumbitch. You really have this whole thing all detailed out, don't you? You're using those xenomaniacs from world-wide big business to fuel your engine, and this thing really is your engine. Why you sneaky, devious, conniving . . . How in the hell did you ever get the balls to even think of this scenario?''

''I was taught by you, sir.''

''Oh, no you don't sport. This is where the student passes the teacher. I know my strengths and weaknesses better than *Time* does. I'm a good soldier, a good teacher, an excellent field commander, and a pretty good handball player. But I am not a good politician, and despite the strength of my convictions, I am nowhere close to you in salesmanship. I may have been a spark on the tinder, but Scotty you have turned into a fucking thermonuclear fireball.''

''Colonel, look at it this way. We were taught the two most important things for a leader to do are, first and foremost the mission; and concurrently, but second to mission, the welfare of the troops. It's your job to take care of the mission—just do it. It's my job to take care of the welfare of the Board and the Executive Committee. Your job comes first, and I promise I won't let my job get in the way or impede you from doing yours. You get out in the pucker with a few desperate men and kick ass and take names. I'll see to it that you have everything you need to insure success, and that nothing gets in your way.''

''Yes, sir, Mr. Ingalls.'' Morse proudly snapped a salute to his one-time protégé, now the boss.

CHAPTER EIGHT

Leslie Campbell, attractive without being pretentiously pretty, has confidence; is bright, bitchy; and, except for her unbridled love and loyalty for Scott, is a classic spoiled little rich girl. She has pulled her hair up into a bun with a number two pencil stuck in the center. The coffee table before her is covered with file folders and random papers. The ashtray is filled with cigarette butts, and there is a half cup of cold coffee in front of her. Scott is standing behind the bar which is also covered with folders and papers.

"Okay, ace, we're ready for phase two. You got your military types lined up, now all you need is big business and their big bucks." She lights another cigarette from the end of the one she is finishing.

"That's already working, my dear. I met with the top five men for the steering committee. They are not only sold, but rabid for the concept. Each one of them has been asked to sell two other people, and each one of the second tier to sell two other people, and so on. Seven levels into the networking, we should have over 640 sold. Then I can send the letter and follow up with the close prior to setting a date for Geneva."

Scott pulled out a matrix that identified each target

executive with a picture, graph, and one paragraph capsule of the man.

"Just like that . . . ? Aren't you afraid of second, or third, person reps altering the story?"

"Les, we're not dealing with a random crowd for some cocktail party joke. These men are tops in their fields, and skilled in analysing and communicating information. Besides, I still get my go around with them."

"This is crazy. I'm beginning to think it can really happen."

"Oh, it can happen, hon. In fact, the five key guys have already ponied up seed money; a million each. And they all think we're asking for too little money so they've upped the ante to a million per company."

"Don't let the hogs get to you, Scott. That's an incredible amount of money."

"Yeah, 640 million is more than chump change, but they feel it's the kind of commitment we need to get before we invite anyone onto the Board."

"You could make a bunch of money just with the start-up capital."

"That's one of the things Ben Slade stressed. He's loaning us his Chief Financial Officer to develop the financials, and Chandler Chase is loaning us a money manager to structure the investment portfolio so we don't have to bleed the board for subsequent mission outlays. We have a Swiss bank account as of the day before yesterday. Which is just as well. Even though we can beg, borrow and steal most of the start-up materials and facilities, we need to buy a few things prior to Geneva to properly package and position I.T."

Scott pulled out a file marked ITSTO&E0001 (International Terrorist Suppressors Table of Organization and Equipment file number 0001) and handed it to Leslie.

"What's this?" She opened the file and started to read.

"That, my love, is the Table of Organization and Equipment. It outlines both the management side of the business and the organization of the tactical operations. Everyone knows that in order to be effective one manager can only manage a max of about six people. That's called span of control. The military side of the equation will handle itself because of normal organizational guidelines which have worked since the days of Julius Caesar. With the board however, we need to structure it more like Parliament or Congress. Therefore we have established committees."

Scott pointed to a sheet that listed them.

•Executive Committee to manage first echelon planning, development and operations.

•Budget and Finance Committee to manage the bucks.

•Intelligence Committee to collect information and ferret out missions. Also to maintain the security and prevent compromise.

•Operations Committee to make things run.

•Diplomatic Committee to interface with governments and expand the network.

•Administration and Logistics Committee to manage the administrative and complex logistics demands.

•Long Range Strategic Planning Committee to develop, manage, and forecast the long range planning of I.T.

"Six of the seven committees," Scott continued, "will have no less than four subcommittees to further delegate the work load. Additionally, it will reduce the size of the groups meeting so they can stretch their muscles and not get buried in a room full of egos. The only committee which will not have any subcommittees will be the Executive Committee."

"Scott, this is all getting kind of overwhelming. Aren't you afraid that with all this stuff, you will lose control? You know Calvin's analogy about Doctor Frankenstein and his monster is getting more and more likely."

"Cal was both right and wrong in his analogy. I'll concede the monster will be smarter than me. But I don't ever intend to let it get stronger. I will sit as an ex officio member of each committee, and Colonel Morse will sit on both the Intelligence and Operations committees. I always intend to have the bigger stick, babe. Knowledge is strength, and while we go through our drills, we will be collecting an incredible amount of intelligence information on all members of I.T. By the time we get to the first meeting in Geneva, two things will be evident: first, to paraphrase Lyndon Johnson, 'they will rather have I.T. inside the tent pissing out, than outside the tent pissing in;' and, secondly, they will recognize the very real need to be part of I.T. for the simple and basic reason that if they are not in I.T. they are out of I.T. These men will intuitively recognize the potential strength of this organization, and they will fight to position themselves within the I.T. structure for reasons of ego, profit, and fear."

"Do you ever listen to yourself?" She stubbed out a cigarette in the overflowing ashtray.

"All the time, hon." He pulled out a cigar, exaggerating the motion, and clipped off the end.

"Ya know, Ingalls, the only thing more impressive than your blue eyes and your frightening intellect . . ."

". . . is my balls. More balls than brains Ingalls, that's me." He lighted his cigar.

"I hope we live through this fantasy, fella."

"Believe me, Les, that is top on the list of priorities."

CHAPTER NINE

Jennifer had just finished her clams casino, which she had said were excellent. She dabbed at the corners of her mouth with a starched napkin and noted, "It's good that was one of your priorities. It must be awkward never knowing if you're ever really safe from some assassin."

"Awkward, but not unbearable. One adjusts."

"I don't know if I could ever adjust to that," added Calvin as he finished his last oyster.

"Well, pal, if you still have aspirations for 1600 Pennsylvania Avenuc you may have to adjust," said Scott.

"It's not the same and you know it," countered the Senator.

"It most certainly is the same, fella. The only difference is you become the selected target by merit of a national vote. The dangers are just as real, and you can end up just as dead."

"I'm just amazed you were able to keep it all secret as long as you did," said Jennifer.

"We sure didn't keep it secret as long as we wanted. Weeks before word leaked out we found someone in the woodpile we didn't expect or want."

"What happened?" asked Calvin.

CHAPTER TEN

Morse was standing on a small wooden platform in a cinder block square building in the middle of nowhere in West Texas. He wore desert camo fatigues with no insignia, and a big white straw cowboy hat. There were 102 men in the room dressed in the same fatigues with a wide variety of head gear from a Red Sox baseball cap to a fez. There would never be any authorized pictures taken of I.T. individuals or groups, so the cadre decided that for the first briefing they would wear their own distinctive headgear. It was fun, and the guys dug it.

"Gentlemen." The room grew quiet as Morse began his briefing. "Before I run down the outline of the field order, I want to thank you all for being here. Don't worry, this isn't gonna be one of those lectures, just a quickie to let you know that we are all in exceptionally good company in this room. We are supposed to be the best in the world and we are the 'good guys.' We have one standing order which will remain constant regardless of the variety of missions we conduct and that is: 'Kick ass and take names!'

"I want to call on each member of the staff to brief the cadre, then I'll outline the order. XO, you lead off. Introduce yourself, your background and job, then your staff."

Morse stepped off the platform, sat down and slipped the big cowboy hat to the back of his head.

"Thank you, Colonel." Sidney Bullerwell stepped up onto the platform wearing a heavily soiled jungle cap with a long visor in front and in back, and made a quick assessment of the men. He was five feet ten inches, about 170 pounds, had black hair and green eyes. He had a short deep scar that ran perpendicular to his left eyebrow literally cutting it in two. "For those who do not know me, I am Major Sidney Bullerwell. I'm thirty-nine years old. I was born and raised in Yorkshire, England, attended Sandhurst, graduated with my commission and went to the commandos, then SAS. I served one tour in Northern Ireland performing very uncommando type tasks. I subsequently resigned, left England for Rhodesia where I joined the Army and was provided with ample opportunity to perform very commando type tasks. I am here as Executive Officer of I.T. and as such shall function as chief of staff for the sections. I'm also number two man. Should Colonel Morse be removed from the scenario, I shall assume command and responsibility for the welfare, discipline and tactical deployment of the units. I would now like each officer to come in order of G-1, thru G-5, and Command Sergeant Major. Introduce yourself to the room and brief your material on Operation Floss. I will be followed by Captain Cachon." With that he came to attention and stepped off the platform.

"Thank you major." Victor Cachon floated up onto the platform, Brasilia police cap on his head, standing tall, but not at attention as he spoke. "Please, forgive my English. I am Victor Cachon, a Captain in the Air Force of Brasil. I am a pilot, but spend most of my time commanding the paper work of the squadron, which is I guess why I get this job. My full time job in Brasilia was as police detective. I am very flattered and excited about being with you very special men in 'I.T.' Rather than speak to the details of Operation Floss, because G-2 has all the intelligence we have so far, and G-3 has all the plans for how we will use the intelligence, I will explain how you will fight the battles of the paper and reports so that we can kick the donkey and get his name."

Cachon reviewed the formats for reports and messages. They were basic and he had kept them simple. There may have been more than they needed but at least they had forms for reporting on who, what, where, when, and how. There were patrol reports, reconnaissance reports, casualty reports, and logistics reports. All reports would be tapped out on a small, hand held computer pad, encrypted electronically and sent in speed bursts for deciphering at the place of receipt. The entire CEOI (Communications Electronic Operating Instructions) were digitized and programmed to respond to voice prints or a thumb print. It would be virtually impossible to compromise even an authentication table.

". . . and each section will be required to submit a daily summary of section activity to the Major not later than 1800 hours. I will be followed by Captain Kapstein."

Jerry Kapstein was always smiling. He was only five eight but had a weight lifter's body—large upper body, small waist, and inordinately thick wrists. He had rusty red hair and a face full of freckles. He had a casual yet very competent air about him. He exuded confidence. He wore a yarmulke.

"Hi, I'm Jerry Kapstein, Captain. I'm still under forty years old—for another two months. I was born in Medford, Massachusetts; went to West Point School for Boys on the Hudson, class of 68; spent two years wearing the green for Uncle; graduated from IOBC, Jump School and Ranger School; became a citizen of Israel in 1971 in time to help defend the only piece of desert without oil under it; had a lot of combat time; and, participated in the Kampala raid. I'm the G-2, Intelligence officer for I.T. My section gets to collect field intelligence from an incredible variety of sources. We have access to most of the intelligence data generated by NATO forces, my friends in the Mossad, and a host of world-wide business intelligence which is proving to be as comprehensive and surprising as the more conventional results of espionage. Here's what we have so far on Operation Floss. Lights, please.'' Someone turned off the lights and Kapstein picked up a remote control unit to key a video tape player.

''This is a satellite photo of the target site.'' He proceeded with the details of which buildings were which; where troops were billeted; physical security measures; avenues into and out of camp; and, locations of air conditioning ducts, sewage drains, water, generators, and communications.

''Once the assault force leaves the Objective Rallying Point, each team will function pretty much autonomously. I'll let Lieutenant Colonel Xing explain the organization and team missions, but I'll outline the anticipated danger areas. He will explain how we intend to eliminate the threats and hit the targets. The routes leading in and out are lousy with seismic intrusion devices, so a land approach is out, although there will be a diversionary airdrop to draw away their first team reactionary force. The towers have 50 caliber machine guns and sagger missiles. The communications shed has the capacity to jam most communication devices, even the KY38's, and guidance systems. They apparently have segregated various weapons into several small armories rather than one central building. We have identified what is where as indicated by this overlay. It will be very important that all secondary targets—weapons, communications and billets—all get hit simultaneously.

"The primary target is this building. It houses the biological warfare unit. Here is a schematic of that building. You will note that although it looks like a single story cement block building, it has a large basement and two subbasements. The ground floor is primarily administrative. The first basement is R & D, and the bowels are largely storage.

"We will remain here, in isolation, as will the assault team when they arrive tomorrow. I have prepared area studies for all of you which are being passed out now. However, we don't intend to be on the ground long enough for you to play with the flora or fauna.

"All field gear will be sterile—no markings—and no one will carry any identification, rings, chains, or good luck charms. Everyone will be issued an identical digital watch presynchronized. We will use several routes to the ORP, with checkpoints to be given just prior to lift-off. I will have detailed dossiers prepared for the assault teams on the key cadre personnel on the target site. If you have any questions, or think of any in the next day or so, please see me. I will be followed by the guy with the fun job of telling you all how we are going to blow this sucker. Lieutenant Colonel Chung Xing."

Chung Xing walked slowly up to the platform, stopped short of the steps, executed a full gainer with a half twist and landed at attention facing the room. Chung Xing had a flair for the dramatic. He wore the red beret of the Vietnamese Special Forces.

"My name is Chung Xing, LTC. I served for over ten years as an officer in the Special Forces of South Vietnam's former army before my country fell from grace to the filthy hands of the red murderers. I was trained in South Korea with our ROK counterparts, and by the troops of the United States Army Special Forces, 5th Special Forces Group and my honored friend Colonel Morse. Prior to the fall of Saigon, I fled to Thailand and have been training guerrillas in preparation for a return to Saigon. I have the honor and privilege to be heading up G-3. I'll let your immediate superiors outline your teams.

"Now, the concept of the operation: We'll rendezvous at the Objective Rallying Point and fly in aircraft with Libyan markings. Five miles short of the objective, the air assault team will split into five elements. Four aircraft will come in low from the four corners of the compound and take out the towers with TOW missiles. At the break off point, the diversionary element will make an airdrop ten miles to the southwest of the compound and proceed in the direction of the compound. That should set off the SID's and prompt the alert of the rapid reaction forces from the base. The fifth element will land the assault teams who will have ninety seconds to take out their targets. The support teams will start jamming sixty seconds prior to the towers going down and will continue to do so until the assault team leader signals with one green star cluster. Once the area is secured, the Intelligence team will break off and collect whatever data they can while the second assault team handles the primary objective. The first floor will be searched by the Intelligence team and then prepared by the support elements who will plant a thermonuclear neutron bomb which, when detonated later, will both destroy and sterilize the biological agents stored in the second basement.

"The teams will rally at the landing point and be exfiltrated by air. Once airborne, the diversion element will prepare for pickup while a squadron of A-10's make strafing runs on the rapid reaction force moving to intercept the diversion force. From the time we blow the towers to exfiltration should not be longer than ten minutes. The various elements will rally at the alternate Objective Rallying Point and return to the staging area. Once debriefed, I.T. President, Mr. Ingalls, will issue a statement concerning the incident.

"That's the concept, down and dirty. The details of each element are included in the Operations Order Annexes which are being passed out now. We will have a working brainstorming session this evening to discuss strengths and weaknesses, and review contingencies. Please hold your questions until that time. I will be followed by Captain Bond." Chung Xing slowly walked back to his seat to the stares of his colleagues.

William Bond was six feet two inches, about 200 pounds, with golden blonde hair, a deep leathery tan and sky blue eyes that reminded one of frozen nitrogen. He wore an Australian bush hat with one side bent up and pinned to the crown.

"G'day, mates. I'm Willy Bond, Aussie Marines. Born, raised and dazed in the land of Down Under. Most of my military training was in the outback after a life as a rancher. Actually, me dad was the rancher. I drew one tour at Fort Benning in Columbus, Georgia, teaching your Infantry school what a waddi is—that's where I met the good Colonel. I've seen my share of the streets of Belfast, and had one tour with your fifth SF Group in Pleiku back in

'69. I'm the G-4 for I.T., and that means I run the company store. I'm the bloke who has to get everything from pyrotechnics and communication devices to A-10's and a bloody neutron bomb. What fun. Insofar as this Operation goes, here's the drill.

"We'll start with the good stuff first: basic weapon will be the Soviet AK-47. It's a tad heavy, but it has more muscle than the AR15's. Sidearms will be the new Smith and Wesson 9mm with 12 round parabellum clips. Hand grenades will include concussion, frag, and a little Willie Peter. I've thrown in a few dozen thermite jobs for melting down the communication stuff and safes. We have TOW missiles for the gunships as well as 20mm cannons. There are a dozen Dragons, in case any of the buildings are harder than Jerry thinks. The aircraft are Soviet, except for the gunships which are Cobras and two Chinooks. A-10's for the strafing run. One never tested but guaranteed neutron bomb, please don't embarrass me by asking where I got that, and a gaggle of AN/PRC 77's and a few KY 38s. Oh yeah, there's the jamming toys, too.

"Jerry will be happy to know that we just got the okay on both satellite and Blackbird fly overs, six and three hours prior to the mission respectively, so we shouldn't have a repeat of Son Tay. We have enough M1-A1's for running around in the staging area. We have constructed a to-scale mock-up of the compound and surrounding area, and a rehearsal site that Hollywood would love to see. Additionally, I have a menu and facilities that would keep even a bloody navy admiral happy, as well as a more than adequately stocked bar, although the Colonel says we have to go dry 48 hours prior to mission.

"Anything you want or need from insect repellent to parachutes, just ask—I live to serve. Oops, one exception—

I am not a pimp and will not provide birds for anyone regardless of rank, race or politics—until after the mission." He tapped out a cigarette, and lighted it.

"I'll be followed by Captain Jean Paul Ouelette."

Jean Paul Ouelette was five feet eleven inches tall, running to the thin side. He had the long muscles of a swimmer, which in fact he had been. He glided up onto the platform wearing the black beret of the French Foreign Legion.

"*Bonjour, mes amis.*" He paced back and forth across the platform as he spoke. "I am Captain Jean Paul Ouelette. I am a graduate of the Sorbonne, and my father's vineyards in Bordeaux. After a rather boring career as a winemaker, I left the family business and joined the Army. That experience proved both interesting and annoying. In the wake of an embarrassing misunderstanding with a superior I found myself assigned to the French Foreign Legion. That unplanned for career move provided me with the opportunity to do a great many very interesting things and meet some extremely interesting people; some very good, some very bad. I am the head of G-5 for our formidable I.T. organization, and as such wear the mantle of Public Affairs Officer. Personally, I have always found it safer to keep one's affairs out of the public and in the bedroom, *n'est-ce pas*? My actual job function will be as the Press Officer of our little group. I will be working very closely with *Monsieur* Ingalls and the good Colonel in determining what we choose to tell the world press about our activities. Most of what I shall be doing will not interfere directly with the rest of the cadre or the operational forces. However, it is important that certain things be understood, and not compromised. Our operations must be considered, at all times, top secret. No one should ever speak of, or even acknowledge, any connection with International Terrorist Suppressors. To do so would most certainly invite retaliation. The only two visible spokespersons for I.T. will be Mr. Ingalls and Colonel Morse. After this first mission, we shall position Mr. Ingalls as an independent spokesperson, not in anyway connected with I.T. He will report to the world press that he had been contacted and paid to report on the activities, but that he knows nothing of the group other than what he receives in the form of communications. In subsequent missions, we may use other independent contractors to report our results and intentions.

"There is a very great danger that despite our efforts we may be compromised at the operational level. Therefore, all I.T. personnel, without exception, shall undergo both polygraph and chemical testing in an effort to ferret out moles. Subsequent to the initial testing, routine, unannounced testing shall occur. Gentlemen, 'death before dishonor' shall become much more than a mere phrase to us all, as well as a newer updated version of death for dishonor.

"Our operational forces have been selected and always will be selected for their talent, ability and skills. We do not care about physical appearances—length of hair, beards. Furthermore, we are less concerned about the form of military courtesy than a conventional force must be. However, although we shall not enforce military appearance or bearing standards, we shall be uncompromising concerning military discipline. Our leaders are the best in the world. It is expected that orders will be executed swiftly and professionally, without question. There will be no 'whys' or explanations. When given an order—do it!

"I shall be followed by Command Sergeant Major Cleveland Rucker."

Cleveland Rucker stood up and actually marched up to the platform. He was five feet six inches tall, 200 pounds, and despite deserving his nickname as the "black brick," he moved with a gracefulness and fluidity which was classic. He had been a first round draft choice by the NFL despite his height because he was frankly the best halfback ever to play in the Pac Ten. He passed on the big bucks and an NFL career when his big brother was killed in Vietnam. He wanted to be a Green Beret but when he learned what Navy Seals were, he immediately went down and enlisted. He finished first in every class he attended, and although he could have had a commission, he chose to pass on that too. He was wearing a Boston Red Sox baseball cap.

"Good morning, gentlemen. I'm Command Sergeant Major Cleveland Rucker. My background is football, the Navy Seals, and some instructor duties. I've been to Vietnam, Grenada, and Lebanon. I've been told that everyone who reports for this mission will be in operational physical condition, and are all professionals like us. My job is to see to it that everyone is in physical condition, and that they are tactically and technically proficient to accomplish the assigned tasks. Colonel Morse selected me for this job because he said I was the only man in this room badder than he is. I intend to prove the Colonel right. You have heard the outline of a daring and demanding mission which, when we get down to it, will lack nothing in planning. My job is to be sure we lack nothing, as far as human resources, to make it happen. Therefore, commencing at 0500 tomorrow morning we start with an eight-mile run and end up in the sawdust pit for some hand to hand refresher work prior to the big breakfast Captain Bond is having prepared. Then we'll link up with the troops and start training for the mission.'' He marched back to his seat and announced as he sat down. ''I will be followed by everyone.''

Colonel Morse hopped back up on the platform and pulled his hat down over his eyes.

''Well done, gentlemen. So much for round one. We will be joined this evening by our boss, Mr. Scott Ingalls. This whole I.T. thing is his brainchild. He put the concept together, and made it happen. Although he won't be involved in the operational portion of this mission, he is just as, if not in some ways, more capable than any of you. I want to brief back to him this evening prior to the planning session. It will be the only dog and pony show you will ever be subjected to while under my command. Now, let's retire to the clubhouse to get better acquainted—the bar is open.''

CHAPTER ELEVEN

It was 0245 hours when there was a loud rap at the door of Jesse Morse. He was sleeping lightly on top of a sleeping bag laid out on an old army cot, a single white sheet covering his large muscled body.

"Yeah?" He was immediately awake and throwing off the sheet.

"Colonel, Kapstein here."

"Come on in, Jerry." Morse rose from a sitting position on the side of his bed and stretched like a panther.

"Sorry to bother you sir, but I think we might have a mole."

"Don't ever apologize for doing your job, Jer. Who? And how the hell did he last this long?" In his undershorts he walked over to the small refrigerator and took out a large bottle of orange juice.

"Ya want some?" When Kapstein indicated no, Morse drank straight from the bottle. He walked over to the table and straddled one of the chairs so he could lean on the back. "All right G-2. I'm awake. Talk to me."

"Bill Devens, sir. The young black-haired guy from Wyoming."

"What about him? If I remember, he was an Eagle

Scout, a rodeo rider, and served with the Marines Force Recon."

"Yeah, that's what's in his jacket, but somehow we think he got switched."

Morse's expression changed from one of quiet interest to furrowed concern.

"He was tested and in-processed at our Utah site. He passed all the physical stuff as well as the polygraph and the Sodium Pent session. His fingerprints, as well as his dental records, checked with the records. When we random spot checked troops here a few weeks back, he again passed the polygraph test. But the guy in the infirmary is not Bill Devens."

"Go on, Captain, I'm still listening," said Morse as the intensity of his stare impaled Kapstein.

"Sir, Devens took a fall off a tower in a free climbing exercise, busted his leg and lacerated his tricep. Well, he was medivaced and put in the infirmary. When Doc ran the normal routine tests it was discovered that his blood type is A Positive." He paused for a moment and then continued.

"Bill Devens' blood type is A Negative."

"Could it be a clerical error?"

"No way, sir. His Marine records show A Negative. His initial physical shows A Negative—but the guy lying in building 1492 definitely has blood type A Positive."

"Speculation?"

"The only reasonable scenario, short of a medical miracle which has a man changing blood type in his sleep, is more than a little disturbing for a whole bunch of reasons. Someone, or some agency, targeted Bill Devens as a prospect for our group—which means they know about us or want to know about us—prepared a clone with plastic surgery, training, and mucho detail, switched bodies prior to departure for this base and planted their mole. Which also means we can assume they know what we are doing, where we are, and who the bulk of us are."

"We're moving. Scramble the troops and cadre, send Bullerwell and Xing to the alternate site QG/8/85 in Arizona. I want this site sterilized and empty in twelve hours. Let me put on some pants, and then let's visit Devens' double. Does he know he's been exposed?"

"No sir, and we've kept him lightly sedated."

Morse pulled on a pair of fatigue pants, a tan T-shirt, and pair of shower thongs. Then he walked over to his bedside table and took out a 44 magnum Ruger Redhawk with a seven inch barrel which he tucked in the waistband of his pants, against the small of his back.

The Devens double was lying in a hospital bed. There was one medic standing next to his bed adjusting the flow of an I.V.

"Is he with us?" asked Morse.

"Yes sir. We're keeping him just on the brink of La-La Land."

"Prepare the sodium pentothal and bring him back to reality. He won't like it."

A few minutes later Morse and Kapstein were joined by Ingalls. They shared a pot of black coffee waiting for the young man to revive. The man in the bed blinked his eyes a few times and stared at the men next to him.

"Good morning, sir." The man smiled. The smile slowly faded and he looked confused as he saw who was looking down on him.

"Good morning," Morse said as he took a step to the side of the bed.

"Son, I'm not in the habit of repeating myself, so listen

real good. We know you are not Bill Devens. We know that sometime after the real Bill Devens was processed, you were switched for him. You don't have the same blood type as Bill Devens, and further investigation during your little nap has shown that you also don't have his fingerprints, or match his dental work. I want you to tell me who are are; who you work for; how you compromised Devens; what you did with Devens; and, what your mission is here. I also want names, locations of drops, means of communication—the whole enchilada."

The Devens double tried to look surprised, hurt, confused, and disoriented all at once.

"That shit ain't gonna cut it, pal. If you don't talk, we'll pump you full of enough drugs to open your mind like a goose's lower GI track."

Recognizing it was useless, the man in the bed smiled and started to laugh.

"Colonel, did you really think you could keep this deal quiet forever? I wouldn't be surprised if there were a half dozen others like me in this camp right now. I realize I'm a dead man whether I talk or not so you can go fuck yourself with a recoilless rifle, honcho man. And you can pump me full of whatever chemical shit you want—it won't work. My mind has been so massaged and fine tuned that even my subconscious was programmed by people who are far better men than any of you cowboys. Anything you get out of me will have to be scraped out with a scalpel. Give it your best shot, guys."

CHAPTER TWELVE

"Don't tell me Morse killed him?" asked Calvin as he swirled his brandy in the snifter.

"Okay, I won't tell you. Anyway, you're messing up the order of the sequence of events," said Scott.

"Scott, how long did you really think you could keep something of that magnitude a secret?" asked Jennifer.

"Only as long as possible. Actually we had originally hoped to keep the entire operation under wraps until after we hit the Libyan site. But that was always a goal, not a realistic objective."

"Goals. Objectives. You sound like a grad student. Can you get back on track before we're raided by the Delta Force or *60 Minutes*?"

"Sure, Cal. I'll get back on track. Is the brandy okay?"

"It's fine. It's your story that has a taste of cork."

"Ah Senator, you turn a phrase like an Erroll Flynn rapier. Remember our fishing trip?"

"I wish I could forget it. It would have made my part in all this a hell of a lot easier."

CHAPTER THIRTEEN

Calvin Pastor was a freshman Senator, but he was still one of the good old boys as far as Washington went. He was one of the rare second generation legislators on the hill, and he used the blessing of that to overcome the curse. He was only forty-two years old but very well thought of by the power brokers who control D.C. politics. He was attractive but physically unthreatening, a characteristic his PR firm fought with him to maintain. He dressed Harvard conservative, and oozed sincerity. However, despite the Clark Kent exterior he was incredibly intelligent, politically ruthless, and inimitably ambitious.

He had agreed to go fishing with Scott for all the right reasons. He needed to get away from the city and the pressure. He enjoyed Scott's company, man to man. He was easy to be with and talk to about nothing. He was also curious. He had seen Scott infrequently since their MBA days at Harvard. Although they might play tennis twice a year and occasionally a round of golf, they never had gone fishing together. Ingalls was also an enigma to Calvin, and that bothered a man who had spent a career being in control. It had also bothered Calvin for years, that Scott never really rose to his potential. Oh, he was making good money running some marketing consulting firm in Boston, but Ingalls could have been in the Senate or more. Ingalls had the spark and charisma which Pastor secretly coveted. They had been close at Harvard, but after graduation when the big business recruiters were a-wooing, Ingalls packs up and joins the Army. Calvin chose instead to go to law school, figuring with an MBA and a law degree he could write his own ticket. And he did.

Meanwhile Scott ran off to slog through jungles and God knows what else playing Green Beret. It didn't compute. After he got out, he did another 180° turn and went to work for a New York ad agency on a soap account, of all things. Calvin kind of lost track of him until he ran for the Senate, when Ingalls sent him a check and an incredibly obscene good luck card. Since the campaign, they had stayed in irregular contact, but purely on a social level—college chums, don't ya know.

Scott walked up to the Arlington home of Pastor and rang the bell. The door was answered by Jennifer Pastor, Calvin's wife of ten years. She was the picture of a healthy-girl-next-door-type Senator's wife. She smiled and kissed Scott's cheek as they shook hands.

"It's good to see you, Scott. Come on in. I'll tell Cal you are here."

"No, don't do that, Jen. Tell him Special Agent O'Keefe from the IRS is at the door and needs to talk to him in private."

She grinned and ran upstairs to deliver the lie.

When the Senator came to the top of the stairs, cheeks flushed, he looked at Scott, then his wife, and laughed as he ran down the stairs.

"Ingalls, not only are you a rotten SOB, but you are a bad influence on my wife."

"Senator, if Jenny can survive ten years with you and

not suffer irreparable damage, my pranks certainly are no danger. Good to see you champ."

"Good to see you, soldier, but you're early. By the way, where are we going? I need to tell my bride, and let my staff know."

"I can give you an eight digit grid coordinate and a radio frequency with time you can chat with them, but we are going into God's country, and that means no street addresses, and no telephones."

"Scotty, you know I'm no good at roughing it." He reached for a pipe off a wall rack.

"Only one night, pal. And besides, once you've been in the wilderness with me, you'll turn your back on Hilton, Hyatt, and Marriott."

"I doubt it," he said as he stuffed tobacco from a silver humidor into his pipe. ". . . those are three heavy campaign contributors you're talking about. Well B'wana, what do I need to bring?"

"Not a thing, Senator, just kiss your wife good-bye. I'll have you back in time for dinner Sunday."

"Gee Scott, this is all very unnatural. A U.S. Senator doesn't just take off into the woods without telling anyone." He relighted his pipe and sucked in heavy blue clouds of smoke.

"Calvin. This is Scott, not the KGB or the goddamn Teamsters. If you can't tear yourself away from the office umbilical cord, that's cool. I'll call you in a couple of weeks. Maybe you can squeeze in a quite safe round of golf or drinks at the club."

"Cal," Jennifer put a delicate hand on her husband's shoulder. "Don't be like one of those old Capitol Hill farts you're always bitching about. Go ahead with Scott. It will be good for you."

"Yeah, I guess you're both right. I can be Capitol Hill farty without even knowing it. Okay, what do I take?"

"Just your leave. I have clothing, fishing gear, and all kinds of good stuff."

"As long as I don't have to jump out of an airplane or eat snake or anything equally vile."

"Senator—trust me!"

"Sure, that means 'fuck you' on the hill."

As they loaded Scott's Avis LTD, Calvin had a flash of deja vu with Scott being in control again and whisking him off in the snow for a ride south on 95 to "visit" his cousin at Pembroke on Providence, Rhode Island's fashionable east side.

"Okay, Scott, why the mystery?"

"Cal, this trip will be good for both of us. Besides which I need to talk to you about something important."

"Are you in some kind of trouble?" It would be a dream come true if he, Senator Calvin Pastor could bail out his old college chum by judicious exercise of his power and influence. In college it had always been Scott who resolved problems, helped those fellow students in need—was generally 'there.' Cal had always been jealous of his friend's ability to solve the unsolvable. If Scott now needed him to get out of some trouble, it would be like the homecoming queen asking you to please be the one to take her virginity.

"Sorry, that's not it. Actually, the opposite is true. You know the axiom 'you're either part of the solution, or part of the problem.' Well, Senator, I propose to be part of the solution."

"That's grand, Scott, but solution to what?"

"I'll wait until we're up in the air. I don't trust any car rented in D.C. not to be bugged by no less than three agencies."

"Bugged smugged, and what do you mean up in the air?"

Twenty minutes later they were in a Beechcraft Bonanza taxiing down the runway. As they were loading the gear into the plane, Scott had outlined the basics of I.T. Calvin didn't respond or comment, but listened. *Time* said he was one of the best listeners in Washington, next to the towel boys in the men's rooms. As the plane leveled out to altitude, Scott dipped a pinch of Skoal and asked the Senator, "Well, what do you think?"

"First, I think that stuff you just put in your mouth is revolting. As to your concept to address terrorism, I think it smacks of vigilantism. Additionally, it inherently violates a myriad of U.S. and international laws. Should you attempt to consummate such an organization I suspect you will be indicted by the State Department, FBI, Treasury, and a passel of state and local departments, not to mention the shit you'll be in with other countries who we all know are less Christian than the red, white and blue."

"Cal, I asked for your opinion because I value it. I should clarify for you that I am serious about this. I spirited you up to 12,000 feet to have you respond to the concept and present your initial SWOT analysis of the concept. Also to solicit your support."

"No way, José. I'll be happy to play devil's advocate for you, but there is absolutely no way I intend to soil my lily whites with this, this—criminal activity. That's what it is you know Scott—criminal. I'm the fair haired boy of D.C., the prodigal son of the former Speaker of the House. At the rate I'm moving I could end up with Ways and Means or even a shot at the White House in another six years. If you want to play jungle rat again go to South Africa, they'd love to have you."

"Okay, Senator, calm down. I'll pass on the support and settle for your analysis of the concept. I'll even abbreviate the drill. I know the strengths and weaknesses as well as the opportunities. That takes care of S, W and O. You outline the threats."

"Scotty, that's the easiest if not the longest task of the exercise. As I see it you have two levels of threats, both equally disconcerting. On the first level, which is the more basic and mundane, you have the various law enforcement and intelligence organizations of the world that will probably view your crusade in a dim if not totally black light. As you explain your plans, you intend to violate jurisdictions of virtually everyone sworn to 'protect and defend.' For the moment, let's forget the state and local jurisdictions and count the federal folks you will piss off: Alcohol, Tobacco and Firearms; FBI, who will no doubt consider you under *both* the Espionage statutes, probably racketeering for good measure. The State Department will be ripped at you doing their job. The Army, Navy, Air Force and Marines will feel slighted. And don't forget your old friends at the CIA who will probably flat out kill you for invading their turf.

"So much for the low level threats. Then you have the biggies. If you didn't learn anything from the movie Frankenstein, consider the analogy. This monster you propose to create will be bigger, stronger, and unlike the Baron's creation, smarter than you. Scotty, I deal with CEO's and international business tycoons every week. One on one, they are bad dudes. You put a couple of dozen of them together . . ."

"A few hundred is more likely," Scott said.

"Oh sure, exc-u-u-u-se me, 'a couple of hundred' of them together and it will be like—remember that time we saw the junk movie with the schools of piranha—well picture the same school of fish, but instead of piranha, substitute great white sharks, and you, my friend, are lunch."

"And what if no one knew I was involved?"

"That would be great, but it's impossible. I know—you'll probably have a couple of hundred others who know also. Do you think you can keep a secret with even three people knowing. Wake up, soldier, you will be world-wide number one target thirty minutes after the first act of your so-called anti-terrorism."

"Cal?"

"What?"

"So I lied." He turned and smiled at the young Senator with a Hollywood white smile.

"You lied?"

"Uh-huh. It's an idea a client has for a movie script, and I just wanted to get some expert input. I appreciate your candor and honesty."

"Why, you rotten little—you know you scared the shit out of me. I mean you're both smart enough and crazy enough to try some half-assed deal like that."

"Naw-w-w. You're too kind, Cal. I might be crazy enough, but I'm not smart enough."

"No, you're smart enough. I just don't think your crazy enough—yet."

The two old friends had a relaxing evening and settled into the campfire with two bottles of Scotch and a box of Oreo cookies. They reminisced, told jokes, and planned the next day's hike to the "special" lake. Halfway through the second bottle of Scotch, Scott asked Calvin, "Ya know that movie script I was telling you about in the plane?"

"Sure, Doc Savage meets Anwar Sadat."

"Well, when the writer finishes it, what kind of men should the hero talk to to smooth over the interagency stuff?"

"You tell your client to imitate life."

Calvin was more than half drunk, and couldn't get out of the camp stool. "Here's the rundown: first, he never goes to political appointees. Naw—get to the career guys, and the heavyweight career guys, GS-16's and above. Start with a guy like Brent Garfield over in State. The new deputy at the Bureau is the next guy—sneaky, ambitious, and knows where all the bodies are buried, literally. ATF ya don't want to cozy up to, so drop down to Regional level and grease that wheel—if ya go to the top with them, ya'll end up with Morley Safer on your doorstep. You'd know the military players better than me, but for sure, you want to include a character like Kissinger. You know, an outsider still on the 'in'—lotsa old favors and personal intelligence information like Hoover's basement. Ya know, Scotty, I'm pretty messed up. How'd we get so drunk?"

"We drunk ourselves drunk, Cal."

"How come I'm drunker than you, huh?"

"Talent, practice and luck, pal."

"Yeah, you always were one lucky SOB." The senator passed out still stuck in the camp chair and with his head against a tree.

The next day they hiked to a small lake nestled in the crotch of three large hills. Scott instructed his old friend in no less than three techniques for taking trout—and they took lots. First they fly fished with Scott talking as he demonstrated. Scott used an old split bamboo eight feet long rod which would have cost over five hundred dollars new, if you could find one. He rigged Cal up with a spinning rod and attached a half full bubble of water to a six feet leader and tied on a fly. They both fished until the morning hatch was over. They released all but two three pounders: one a Rainbow, and one a German Brown. Later, after Scott had cooked the fish over an open fire, they fished with worms and various lures. They paused at lunch time for a candy bar and a short nap on the sun warmed grass.

Cal woke up from his nap when he heard a strange noise. When he opened his eyes he heard Scotts voice, very firm yet almost like a whisper. ''Don't move, Cal. Just lie very still. Shut your eyes for a moment.''

As Cal shut his eyes, Scott moved in slow motion toward the coiled timber rattler not a foot from the resting Senator's head. He moved a walking stick size branch slowly in front of the snake and started to rotate it in small circles. When the snake struck at the stick, Scott snapped his hand out and grabbed the snake behind the head. Cal jumped up at the movement.

''What the fuck?'' he muttered.

''You were apparently lying on his highway to dinner. You annoyed him,'' said Scott.

''What is it? Is it poisonous?'' asked Calvin visibly shaken.

''Oh, yeah. It's poisonous. A timber rattler. A small one though. He wouldn't have killed you, although you would probably have gotten a little sick.'' Scott walked into the woods a short ways and released the snake.

''Why did you do that? Shouldn't we kill it?'' asked Cal.

''Kill it? Why? We invaded his turf. Besides, they eat rats and mice and I hate rats and mice.''

''What about Republican Senators?''

''You've got a point there. Maybe you smelled like a rat to him,'' laughed Scott.

"You son of a bitch."

"So I've been told. Hey, since we're awake how about some more fishing. And please, watch where you step. I don't want you bothering any more of the neighbors."

In the plane on the way back to Virginia, Calvin felt relaxed and oddly refreshed.

"Scotty, this was absolutely first rate. I feel great. You are a top shelf cook, and a primo fishing guide. I didn't even have a hangover."

"Thank you, Senator. We should make it a habit, at least once a year. As for the hangover, I spiked the dessert with B-12."

"Good old B-12. I still think you should have killed that snake."

"He didn't need killing—and you'll probably be wrong again sometime," smiled Scott.

"No doubt. Hey, you know that script your client is working on?"

"Yeah."

"If it would help, send me a copy of the final draft, and I'll punch it up for you from the inside of D.C. perspective. It should really make for an interesting movie. Too bad you couldn't do something like that for real."

"Yeah, too bad. But like Albee said in one of his plays, '. . . what is gained is loss.' "

"Hey, that's a great quote, I've got to remember it for my next speech when the tax bill comes up again. Let me try a pinch of that Skoal shit, and don't you dare tell Jenny or *Time*."

CHAPTER FOURTEEN

"Cal, how could you put that foul carcinogenic in your mouth?" asked Jennifer as she put down her glass and stared at her husband.

"Thanks, Scott. Another political indiscretion exposed," moaned Calvin.

"Sorry, pal. It slipped out." Scott smiled.

"And you say your life depends on security?" asked Calvin.

"And yours depends on not polluting your body. Senator Pastor, that is disgusting," said Jennifer.

"Oh? Buddy boy here throws decapitated heads in the sand and he's a friggin' hero. I let him corrupt me with a dip of snuff and I'm a villain?"

"Hey Jen, look at it as research for his battle against the tobacco lobby. Do you want to hear what eventually happened to our mole Devens?"

"Yeah. Did John Wayne Morse really dust him?" asked the Senator.

"Since you asked," Scott continued.

CHAPTER FIFTEEN

Morse looked blankly down on the malevolent face of the impostor Eagle Scout and was annoyed. "You've told us quite a lot already, sport. But you're right, there isn't any sense in wasting chemicals on a preconditioned piece of small shit like you." With that the Colonel reached behind him and slipped out the Ruger Redhawk.

"You all know how we plug security leaks," he said as he pointed the revolver at a spot above the nose and between the eyes of the infiltrator. ". . . with extreme prejudice!" Morse said as he blew a small hole in the Devens-double's forehead.

"Colonel, look what you've done. Now we need to replace a pillow and a mattress," said the medic.

Morse ordered an emergency staff call to discuss the Devens incident and to outline contingencies during the move to the alternate site, and the subsequent unannounced moves they would execute every three days until the mission date was confirmed.

They all knew that eventually they would be exposed. They also knew that once they started doing business, they would all be targets. However, few of them expected to actually be compromised prior to even pulling off their first mission. Reactions varied from anger to confusion and frustration. Kapstein was depressed that despite all his measures it could have happened.

"If only I had run the full battery of confirmation checks when the troops landed here, we could have caught him eight weeks ago," he kept saying.

"Jerry," countered Morse, "look at the bright side. He snuck in, and went through training—but he stayed in isolation with the rest of us. He couldn't have passed anything to anyone. No communications can get out of the camp because of jamming devices. No one could breach our perimeter because of the intrusion devices. There are no phones—no one could have talked to anyone outside."

"Sir, there are two inaccuracies in what you say: first, he didn't need to get out or communicate electronically or telephonically. What if he had a simple code employing signals—small panels laid out in the desert to be read by air?"

"There have been no flyovers since we arrived except for Mr. Ingalls plane."

"Colonel, if someone could condition that guy's mind to last through truth serums and sophisticated interrogation they could also have access to satellites or high altitude reconnaissance aircraft like a U-2 or Blackbird," said Kapstein.

"Aw shit . . ."

". .. and the other point is two-fold: there has been air traffic here, and not everyone has been in isolation. Mr. Ingalls has been in and out four times since we landed here."

"You're out of line, Captain." Morse rose to his full height.

"At ease, Colonel," said Ingalls. "Jerry is not out of

line. He is doing his job. And his job means—has to mean—that no one person gets treated or considered any different than any other person. Hell, if someone could switch a relatively insignificant soldier like that, you bet your jump wings they could try the same thing with me or even you, Colonel.'' They all looked at each other strangely.

''Colonel, here are your orders: first, retest me—polygraph, chemicals, blood, dental records, fingerprints. Make provisions for doing the same to the entire operational force on a routine but irregular schedule. Appoint one man per section with the official task of sharpshooting the section leader. We need many more why's, what if's, and how comes, at the staff level. We don't allow that at the troop level, but with the planning and security of I.T., every decision needs to be SWOT analyzed, dissected, countered, and sterilized. Gentlemen, in a few days you will be flying several thousand miles to kill a couple of hundred men, detonate a neutron bomb in the desert of Libya, and return safely to fight another day. Our job is to fix mistakes. Inherent in that job is a quest for the ideal. We simply cannot make mistakes.''

Everyone was paying very close attention to Ingalls when Willy Bond asked, ''But who the bloody hell planted the Devens deal?''

''Time answers all questions,'' said LTC Xing. ''It was the first time, but no doubt will not be the last. It matters not what drove the tiger into your trap—just that he is captured and killed before he can kill you.''

''Amen!'' said Ouelette.

''Let's get outta here. We have to pack everything up and be loaded by 1900 hours,'' ordered Morse as they all start to pick up materials on the table and moved toward the door. Scott Ingalls and Jerry Kapstein remained behind. Kapstein looked at Ingalls with an uncharacteristically embarrassed gaze.

"Come on, Jerry, we got a date. And remember—don't ever apologize for doing your job well. After we're through, I want you to give this Devens situation a top priority. We need to know who put him in here, and how." He put his arm around the shorter man's brawny shoulder.

"Scott, we are turning into some kind of paranoid bunch of sumbitches, aren't we?"

"Jer, with this group, paranoia is more than a symptom—it's a job requirement. Let's go do it." The President of International Terrorist Suppressors walked off with the Intelligence officer to undergo interrogation.

CHAPTER SIXTEEN

Ben Slade was having his first prospecting meeting on the top floor of the Harvard Club in Boston. He sat in the lounge by the window with an impressive view of Back Bay and parts of the Boston skyline. Ben was a former cabinet member under the Kennedy administration, and currently CEO of one of Detroit's cornerstones. He believed in the I.T. concept and was meeting with a counterpart from the steel industry to sell him on the concept.

Similar meetings were taking place all over the world among similar type men. Men of power, reputation, and conviction.

Chandler Chase, head of the second largest bank in the country, was meeting the Chairman of an oil company in Dallas. Remington Danforth, CEO of one of the largest brokerage houses in the world, was meeting on Nob Hill with the head of the Rice CoOp. Ross Lasser was trying to buy out Metromedia while he met to discuss I.T. with the number three man of Triad on a Lear jet crossing the Atlantic. Byron Moore got in on the ground floor in Silicon Valley and intended to do the same with I.T. He was meeting with a Japanese business patriach on a yacht off Cabo San Lucas. And so on, and so on, and so on.

CHAPTER SEVENTEEN

Scott had chosen Newport, Rhode Island as the site for the first meeting of the Executive Committee for a variety of reasons. The idea was conceived in Newport and he felt it appropriate to move into this phase here. He loved the area and had a sentimental attachment to it. An at sea meeting was private and eliminated certain security considerations.

They were meeting at Goat Island, to board a chartered yacht. Within three hours everyone would get limo rides to private planes and be gone.

"Gentlemen, thank you for taking time from your busy schedules to meet today. We will be pulling out in a few minutes. Please note the agendas in the folders in front of each of you. Basically, we have two objectives: first, to update one another on progress thus far; and, second to charge you men with the task of developing the bylaws so that they can be presented in Geneva. Subsequent to your briefings, we will also establish a realistic and attainable timeline leading to a fixed date for the seminar in Geneva. This collection of talent covers most of the key bases necessary for the Executive Committee: automotive manufacturing; banking; brokerage; communications; and, high tech. Additionally, we will learn this afternoon that we also have commitments from oil, shipping, airlines, steel, agriculture, medicine, and the orient. As we pass the Inn at Castle Hill I will point out a spot about 600 yards off shore from the lighthouse as the place where I actually crystalized the idea of I.T. I will ask you all to join me in a toast to that spot of water; to our future; and, the potential impact we can all have on the future.

"Gentlemen, it is my very great pleasure to introduce you all to a friend, my mentor; the man who will lead our operational forces, Colonel Jesse Morse, United States Army Retired." Scott indicated Morse to his right.

"Gentlemen. It is a very great honor to be part of this group. I am here to listen, and to swear to you the unbridled efforts of my talent, experience and knowledge. If you men provide the means and the form, I guarantee you the substance and the results we all crave." The lords of business looked intently at Morse, then almost in unison solemnly nodded.

The seventy-two foot yacht just cleared the tip of Jamestown when Ben Slade started talking.

"I've had private talks with my counterparts at other Detroit auto plants and, with the exception of General Motors who are routinely conservative and bogged down in more committees and bureaucracy than the government, everyone is in, as long as we can guarantee anonymity. We have all agreed that the million dollar initiation would be buried in R & D. Likewise, the folks I talked to in the steel industry are with us." Ben went into the details of each of his meetings, highlighting the amusing and salient points.

Chandler Chase was next up.

"You've got the backing of the banks, and the new

entries into national finance to include Sears and Merrill Lynch. Remmy no doubt has more to add from his meetings.'' He poured himself another glass of wine.

Even in his casual attire, Remington Danforth looked like an ad for Brooks Brothers, complete with golden fleece logo.

''Well, obviously, I'm in and so are the other houses listed on my summary sheet. I picked up a bonus on the golf course when I felt out the head of one of the big eight accounting firms. Not only did Thaddeus go for it, but he set up meetings for me with the others, and as of today we have solid commitments from six of the eight. They all see it as good for business and influence peddling. Again, though, they want to be kept strictly sub rosa.''

''Mr. Danforth, I can guarantee they will be so far under the rose, they'll get a crick in their neck just to see the roots,'' said Scott as he waded through the file folders in front of him.

''I had fair luck with my prospects,'' said Ross Lasser. ''Although, personally, I think that some of the network honchos might try to gain an advantage exploiting I.T. Especially some of the new young Turks.''

''You mean guys like you, Ross?'' quipped Slade.

''Oh, don't worry about me, Ben. I believed Scott when he tactfully intimated that security leaks could be fatal. He left it open enough not to be subtle.'' He wasn't smiling when he said it.

''Ross, we shouldn't have a problem. In fact, we're going to need their early support in communicating to the world press. And you know I would never do anything to hurt any of you. You are all much too important to us. This entire concept is based on the premise of mutual exploitation.''

"Ross is only kidding, Scott," said Chase. "He knows, as we all do, that you would never do anything like that." He poured himself more coffee and added "You'd get Colonel Morse to arrange it." They all laughed, if somewhat uneasily.

Byron Moore was the youngest man in the group being two years younger than Scott. He was fit, tanned, and genuinely handsome with chiseled features and clear probing eyes.

"You've got all the important computer companies, and most of the Oriental concerns. Of course, the Japs don't trust the Koreans, who don't trust the Chinese, who don't trust anyone. But the Chinese are so desperately hungry for technology, and the form of 'belonging' that they literally jumped at the opportunity—insofar as the orientals jump at anything."

"Gentlemen, this is truly outstanding. What does that leave us with right now." He turned to Leslie who was synthesizing the data from each man's summary report.

"Well, Mr. Slade has hard commitments from nine businesses; Mr. Chase has eleven positives and four tentatives; Remmy has a whopping fourteen carved in granite; Mr. Lasser counts ten; and, Byron lists sixteen for sure. That's fifty-four as of now." She recounted the lists.

"Criminy. That's more than five times what we needed for this phase."

"Scott, you are to be congratulated. If this doesn't happen, I have a job for you soon," said Chandler raising his glass.

"Stand in line, Chase," retorted Slade.

"That's very flattering, gentlemen. But, as I think we can all already see, it is unlikely with this level of support that I.T. isn't going to happen."

Ross Lasser stood up and raised his glass. "Gentlemen, may I propose a toast?" They all picked up glasses and rose to their feet.

"To the success and longevity of International Terrorist Suppressors!"

"And to the men that will make it happen," added Scott.

The remainder of the boat ride out to Block Island, around the island and back was devoted to cleaning up details, additional networking, and establishing plans for the meeting in Geneva.

"Gentlemen, Leslie and I will develop an itinerary for me so I can follow up the men already contacted. You men must now undertake the task of drafting the bylaws for us to present at the meeting." Scott fished out a cigar from a humidor.

"Scott, give me one of those Jamaican ropes," said Danforth. "We can probably bang out your bylaws in a weekend at my place in Palm Springs. However, in all candor, I don't think we need to have you take the extra time to pitch it to the host. We're no longer talking about prospects, son, these businesses have been pitched already, and closed. You concentrate on the tentatives and marginal folks. We can be collecting interest on the money of the businesses which have already committed long before we get to Geneva."

"I agree with Remmy," added Slade.

"Me too," Chase said.

"Likewise," shouted Lasser.

"It's unanimous, pal," said Moore. "You've got the order. Shut up and go on to the next task."

"Who am I to argue with my Executive Committee?"

"Don't be coy, lad," sneered Slade. "None of us doubts you are capable and willing to argue with us. But this time, don't."

After the business leaders of the nation loaded into limousines and were off, Scott, Colonel Morse and Leslie returned to the boat.

"Those guys are something else," Leslie said in a stage whisper as she locked the case containing the files into the safe.

"They didn't get where they are by being lightweights, lady," said Morse.

"It was an outstanding meeting. Les, what are you doing?" asked Scott, with a look of concern.

"Locking these files up. What does it look like?"

Scott and Morse exchanged glances.

"Leslie, that is one big aw shit for you."

"What for?" she pouted.

"Les, as you deal with these documents, security is paramount. We just walked off the boat and to the dock; spent fifteen minutes in the parking lot; and, returned. Those documents should have been locked up prior to our ever leaving. I don't know whether to be angry with you or me for not catching it. Check those files right now." She opened the case. The file folders, were full of blank pages.

"Oh, my God," she cried, and tears started running down her cheeks.

"Not to worry, folks, but we wanted to make a point," said Jerry Kapstein as he emerged from the forward cabin, metal attache in one hand, a nine millimeter in the other. "I've got the files, and the tapes of your meeting."

Scott looked at Morse who smiled and shrugged.

"Always have a backup, sport. It never hurts," chanted Colonel Morse.

"Colonel, thank God," Scott started to say.

"Thank him for those gents who exceeded their goals by 500%, Scott. I just hope my side performs half as well."

Morse opened a bottle of champagne and handed a glass to Leslie. And the four of them, Scott, Leslie, Morse, and Kapstein sat down to kill a bottle of Dom Perignon.

CHAPTER EIGHTEEN

It was 0245 hours when there was a loud rap at the door of Jesse Morse.

"Yeah?" he called out immediately awake and throwing off the sheet.

"Colonel, Kapstein here."

"Come on in, Jerry." Morse rose from a sitting position on the side of his bed and stretched like a panther.

"Sorry to bother you, sir, but I think we might have a mole."

"Don't ever apologize for doing your job, Jer. Who and how the hell did he last this long?" In his undershorts he walked over to the small refrigerator and took out a large bottle of orange juice.

Calvin said, "You told us that part already. Morse killed the kid and Kapstein retested you. What about the 'Unholy Alliance?' I still can't believe those guys ever actually got together."

"Well, you now know for a fact from your own Committee's report that they did. But first, let me backtrack a bit. I left out something that might help you, or at least your darling wife."

"What's that, Scott?" asked Jennifer.

"An insight I gained from Leslie. It went like this."

* * *

Leslie sat on the couch with stacks of files overflowing with computer runs surrounding her. Her hair was pushed into a bun with the inevitable pencil sticking out the top like an Iroquois Indian's feather. She had just opened her second pack of More cigarettes of the day and it wasn't even noon yet. In front of her, on the coffee table, was a half finished cup of coffee, gone cold. She had taken off her glasses and was rubbing her eyes with her fists when Scott walked in.

"Hi, pretty lady. How goes it?" he asked.

"I'll say this for you, blue eyes. You are a prolific fucking writer. If half this shit really can be done I.T. is going to be busier than Bloomingdales the day after Christmas."

"Well, that's your area of expertise. Anyway, what I've tried to do is anticipate every potential eventuality in which a terrorist group might strike and develop generic contingency operations plans. The details of time, place, air movements and so forth can be inserted, but by having the contingency plans we can save a lot of time in planning which can speed up our reaction time and make us a for real immediate action operation."

"I am having a little trouble with some of this stuff," Leslie moaned.

"How so? You always said I wrote with a fair amount of clarity."

"Sure, this stuff if real clear if you understand the language. But for a lowly civilian like *moi*, it's clear as mud. I am especially confused by the MFI which seems to permeate every thing you write."

"MFI?" he asked.

"Yeah. MFI—more fucking initials."

"Oh!"

"Let me see. 'O.' That's the letter between 'N' and 'P' isn't it? Look Scott, when I went to Europe the first time, I took a Berlitz course so I could at least ask *'Ou est la salle de bains?'* When I did that research project for Senator Allan they gave me a glossary of terms used by the Nuclear Reglatory Commission. It would sure help if you guys could tell me what the fuck a FEBA, ORP, LD, and all that other initialed shit is." She took out another cigarette and lighted it from the butt of its predecessor.

"Sorry babe. You know all businesses have their own jargon, and the tendency is to assume that everyone you are dealing with knows what you are talking about. I forgot you wouldn't understand our tactical terms—for that matter most of the Board is probably lost too. Tell you what, I'll give you a thumbnail rundown of terms right now, and have Bullerwell compile a glossary of terms for you and the Executive Committee as well.

"That would be just ducky, love."

"Okay, lady, here we go with Ingalls 'Tactical Terms 101'. We will acquaint you with the terms of defense and concentrate on small unit tactics, especially Raids and Ambushes."

"Should I take notes or get popcorn?" asked Leslie.

"Neither. I already told you, you will have a glossary to refer to. First, generally speaking, we will at all times attempt to employ the three basic elements to any ambush in all our missions. They are Surprise, Firepower, and Violence of Action. Doctrine prescribes that in most cases one should attempt to achieve a three to one superiority in force size. Therefore, a ten man terrorist squad would be attacked by a thirty man platoon."

"What if you get attacked?" she asked.

"We will not be engaged in any defensive operations, but you will need to know defensive terms insofar as we define the Objective. I'll give you some Fort Benning texts which outline the schematics of a defensive position."

"Oh goody! Just what I need—homework assignments."

"You will note a lot of detail on movement plans—air movement plans, ground movement plans, naval movement plans. They all have a few things in common, and a few things unique. We will never move in a straight line from point to point. There will be series of doglegs. At each turn we designate a Checkpoint. There will normally be two routes planned to an Objective and two routes leaving—a Primary and an Alternate for each. None of them will be the same. The last Checkpoint prior to an assault is called the Objective Rallying Point because it is the Rallying Point just prior to the Objective. This is usually referred to as the ORP."

"Not to be confused with the Subjective Rallying Point, right?"

"Les. . . ."

"Okay, okay. I'm sorry. Go on, teach." She leaned forward in exaggerated interest.

"The sequence of movement for an assault element will normally be: a) Isolation Area—the place where the troops are briefed, plan and rehearse; b) Assembly Area—not to be confused with Alcoholics Anonymous—the final staging area from which movement is started; c) Line of Department—the geographic line which is the starting gate for the movement; d) Check Points—not to be confused with Command Post which is also called CP—Check Points are usually the turns in the dogleg routes to and from an objective, although they may be prominent topographic pieces of terrain. They are distinguished from the Command Post by adding a suffix as a designator of the exact location. The suffix maybe a color, a letter, or a number—CP Red, CP Charlie, or CP02. If we use colors for the tours to the Objective, I normally use letters or numbers for the return suffix.''

''You better be careful with colors. I happen to know you're color blind.''

''Point noted,'' he said as he continued.

''e) Command Post—the office in which the bosses work; f) Landing Zone—a designated landing place for aircraft; g) Drop Zone—a designated place for the landing of troops or equipment by parachute; h) Objective Rallying Point—already described as the last checkpoint and rallying point prior to the assault. It is at the ORP that the final leaders reconnaissance will take place and final orders be given; i) Objective—OBJ—the target or final destination of the mission.''

''I hate to admit it, but it's all very logical. Are you sure this is Army shit?'' she asked.

He ignored her comment as he continued. ''You will also note that military correspondence suffer from an unbridled license which results in assigning anagrams to previously undesignated terms. Rather than refer to a dead letter drop—which is a place where messages can be left and recovered without making direct contact with a messenger—it may be referred to as DLD Orange. Again colors, letters, or numbers serve as a suffix to further identify the exact location. Radios and certain pieces of equipment will also have lettered names. Rather than Motorola or Sony, radios may be ANPRC/77's (which stands for Army Navy Portable Radio Communications, the 77 is the model number. You'll become familiar with most of the other terms through use and being around them. If you hear or read a term you don't understand, ask. Most of the terms are very logical once you know the keys. A LAW is a Light Antitank Weapon. The FEBA you referred to earlier is the Forward Edge of the Battle Area. Remember, if you don't understand a term, ask. No one will think any less of you for it."

"Hey Teach, how about TOFFA?" Leslie asked with a smile.

"Okay. I'll bite. What's TOFFA?"

"Time Out For Foolin' Around."

"I don't normally fraternize with the students, but in your case, I'll make an exception. He leaned forward to pluck the pencil out of Leslie's hair. As he did she started to unbutton his shirt and bite his shoulder.

"Ouch. Careful—you'll scar me for life." He smiled.

"Sounds good to me." She pulled him down onto the couch.

CHAPTER NINETEEN

THE RANGER CONCEPT

Ranger training is realistic, rough and, to a degree, hazardous. It is designed to develop the individual's self-confidence, leadership and skill in the application of basic principles and techniques. Ranger training will teach and train individuals to overcome mental and physical obstacles by using combat realistic situations in small unit tactical exercises. Emphasis is placed on teaching survival and land navigation principles and techniques; the development of good leadership habits through the use of a tactical vehicle—the patrol; developing physical and mental endurance. Ranger (battle) confidence is developed by placing the Soldier in a combat environment where he must learn to survive, move and fight at extended distances behind enemy lines. He must do this with minimum support. Hunger, fatigue and tactical realism will uncover strengths and weaknesses that an individual does not know he possesses. Through Ranger training, he gains an insight into himself and his fellow Soldier.

—from FM21-50 RANGER TRAINING AND RANGER OPERATIONS, Headquarters, Department of the Army, January 1962

CHAPTER TWENTY

At 0455 hours, the cadre of the I.T. operational force was milling around outside the command building when CSM Rucker marched up. As he was spotted, the men started to put out cigarettes and cigars. They were all clad in desert fatigues and field caps. He stood facing the group and shouted, "Fall in!"

The cadre, including Colonel Morse and Scott Ingalls, all stood at attention, head and eyes fixed ahead.

"Good morning, gentlemen," he barked.

"Good morning, Sergeant Major," they all shouted in unison.

"We've all had an evening of briefings and a good night's sleep. Now, let's get those cobwebs out and see what kind of shape all you heroes are in. Open ranks—march. Extend to the left—move. Arms downward—move. Right—face. Extend to the left—move. Arms downward—move. Okay folks—let's do it. Forward—march. Double-time—march."

The troops were off on their first, although certainly not their last, eight mile run with the stoic "Black Brick."

Fifty-six minutes later, sweating profusely, they came back to the command building.

"Quick time—march. Detachment—halt. Left—face. Assemble to the right—move. At ease." There was a lot of sweating, a little heavy breathing and a herd of smiles.

Rucker faced the man and appeared not even to be breathing hard. However, his face was covered with sweat and his T-shirt was soaked. "Not bad, gentlemen. We averaged seven minute miles. Now, let's march to the sawdust pit for some contact sport," he barked and almost smiled. "Atten—shun. Right—face. For ward—march. Double-time—march."

They ran another mile to the sawdust pit, stopped, paired off for warm-up throws and counters. They practiced their arts for about thirty minutes, changing partners every ten minutes.

"Okay, gentlemen," Rucker announced. "Now a quick game of shark-in-the-cage and we can clean up and have that big breakfast."

Shark-in-the-cage consists of one man surrounded by six other men. He goes one fall with each of the six men. There were 120 men present so they had seventeen "cages" going. When they were done Rucker walked into the pit.

"All right men. We still have a few minutes, so we'll have a quick round of King-of-the-Pit. The top man from each cage step forward."

The top seventeen men were colonel Morse, Scott Ingalls, Sidney Bullerwell, Jerry Kapstein, Chung Xing, Jean Paul Ouelette, MSG Robert Wayne, Amid Rashadd, Bennie Wood, Randolph Yee and seven others.

"The rules are simple, you all know them. Once a man is thrown down, he's out. Last man standing wins. If you don't mind, I'll join in to round it out. However, we have to tame it down a bit. So, no breaking bones, and no fatal blows. Begin."

It was mayhem. Immediately Kapstein and Wayne charged

Rucker from opposite sides. Wayne went down to a *tai otoshi*; Kapstein caught an elbow in the gut and was foot swept to his butt. Scott dropped Rashadd and Wood quick with a full roundhouse and wrist technique. Morse took out Yee by sheer muscle. Xing nailed Bullerwell while the latter was looking for an unengaged target. As one man attempted to throw an opponent, two men blind sided him to the chrunch of a dislocated knee. Elsewhere bodies are flying, falling, and bleeding. Thirty seconds into it the combatants backed off to survey who was left: Morse, Ingalls, Xing, and Rucker remained. Scott turned on the smallest man, Xing. That was a mistake. His first two techniques were countered and he found himself lifted by the belt and collar by the smaller man and literally thrown from the pit, landing on his back in an almost adequate judo fall. Rucker blindsided Xing, dropping him in a heap. The two remaining were Morse and Rucker. They stalked each other like two wild cats. Rucker exploded with a flying reverse roundhouse that Morse tried to counter by sweeping his leg by. However, the force of the counter sent Rucker in a complete 360° turn and he connected into the Colonel's floating ribs but without full force. Morse attacked with a side kick; countered by Rucker who followed up with a solid elbow to the midsection that wobbled the Colonel, who then attempted to counter with a series of horse stance straight punches that succeeded in driving Rucker back. The two men smiled at one another—the first real smile anyone had seen on Rucker's face—as Morse snapped another side kick which Rucker stepped under, at the same time grabbing Morse's planted leg by the ankle, pulling with one arm while snapping a punch into the bossman's unprotected ribs with the other, dropping him like a tree.

"You still got it, Sergeant Major," Morse said sitting on his butt trying to catch his breath.

"Yes, sir. Always had it—still got it—never lost it. You did very well, sir." He helped the Colonel back to his feet.

He marched back to the podium to collect his blouse as the cadre brushed off sawdust, sweat and a little blood.

"Well done, gentlemen. Let's get cleaned up and have breakfast. Then prepare to meet the troops."

Standing in the shower, Scott turned to Morse. "Where the hell did you find Rucker?"

"Kinda impressive, isn't he?"

"That's an understatement. Talk about the right man for the right job. By the way, how do you feel, old man?"

"Nothing but my dignity damaged. Speaking of which, you did okay out there for a civilian."

"I figure, it's important that these men know I'm more than some chair jockey executive. But, having made a point, I think I'll retire. What the hell did Xing do to me anyway?"

"He dropped your young ass is what. He's pretty good at that stuff. Ouch—goddamn it—I think I might have cracked a rib."

"You had some help, Colonel."

"Yeah. Let's get dried up and try to eat something."

"I could eat a horse," Scott said. "I'm not so sure I could keep it down though."

CHAPTER TWENTY-ONE

After a breakfast that rivaled the buffet at the Fairmont in San Francisco, the cadre assembled at the landing strip to greet the troops of the operational force. Morse and Xing had hand picked the 285 men from dossiers prepared by Kapstein's section. They covered a wide spectrum of talent and tactical experience: Rangers; Special Forces; Seals; Marines; Seabees; British Commandos; Israeli paratroopers and desert patrols; Rhodesians; Expatriate Cubans; Former Vietnamese Special Forces; Thais; Chinese; Japanese; Sicilians; Greeks; Legionnaires; and, assorted Soldiers of Fortunc who by accident of history and age were seeking to gain combat experience denied them by history.

Every man had, prior to arriving, undergone the routine testing required. That included grueling physicals, endurance tests, confidence courses, and the mandatory polygraph and chemical testing. The latter had flushed out four KGB agents, who fooled the polygraph but not the chemicals; one IRA operative; and, about a dozen less sophisticated terrorist types from Iranians to black South Africans, even two Zulu tribesmen. This force was relatively secure. Nevertheless, they were told very little about the organization they had joined or exactly what they were going to do except get a chance to fight, and perhaps die. Gradually, they were informed that they were the good guys; that they would be fighting terrorism, although it was never specified for whom. Speculation was constant.

Rucker's schedule of training kept everyone pretty busy— and tired. Despite the grueling prescreening, over sixty men were washed out in the first two weeks for a variety of reasons: several couldn't meet the physical demands imposed by Rucker; two were certified psychotics; three men were such dedicated anti-black bigots that they refused to take orders from a "nigger"— which netted them broken collar bones and a variety of contusions in addition to a plane ride out of I.T.; and, most of the rest simply were not team players and didn't fit into the formula.

Gradually, training moved from just PT and hand-to-hand, to weapons, demolitions, advanced first aid, land navigation, patrolling, and daily TEWT's (Tactical Exercises Without Troops). The TEWT's were played on sand tables in the field, and on computers programed to visually display on a television the results of certain actions.

Eventually, everyone started to notice that the Tactical Reaction Tests in the field and all the TEWT's had started to play the same basic scenario. It consisted of an Airmobile raid on a desert compound. It could have come right out of FM21-50, except it included elements of NBC (Nuclear, Biological and Chemical) warfare. Something no one really liked. It was one thing to face down a 50-calibre machine gun or incoming 82mm mortars, but to get ambushed by Typhoid, Bubonic Plague, Mustard gas or a nuke, was a totally different kind of action.

Eight weeks into training, the troops started seeing officer types in the training area. No one wore insignia or rank, but soldiers can tell. The big white haired guy, with the big shoulders and flat gut, could have worn leotards and there would be no mistake about that bearing, confidence and the way the others reacted to him. He was the boss. Saluting wasn't only not required, it wasn't allowed. The most that was accepted was a thumbs-up sign to acknowledge receipt of an order or signal salutation. Everyone within sight noticed that CSM Rucker, who they were convinced was not human but some robotics experiment, snapped to attention and threw a thumbs-up to the big man. No doubt about it, he was the boss.

That speculation was confirmed one evening when, prior to a night patrol that was to cover ten miles through booby-trapped 'wait-a-minute-vines,' he walked into the assembly area and called off the patrol. Rucker assembled the troops on a set of bleachers next to the sawdust pit, and introduced the mystery man.

"Gentlemen," he began. "We have been training pretty hard so far, and although most of you know better than to ask, everyone is more than a bit curious about what we have been training for. Tonight you find out. For the past eight weeks, I have been your mother, father, wife and primary target. Half of my job is done. You guys are ready. The next half is the dicey part. I will now introduce you to our Commander who will give you all the G-2 you need to know for now, and issue our first for real Frag order. On your feet! Troops, I want you to meet Colonel Jesse G. Morse, Commander of this ragtag collection of dangerous professionals. Colonel." Rucker took two steps back and stood at parade rest.

"At ease, men. Take your seats. Smoke 'em if you got 'em. Gentlemen, I've been a soldier for thirty years. During that time, I have seen a lot and had the pleasure to serve with some truly outstanding fighting men. I have served with some of the most elite forces in the world: 5th Special Forces; 2nd Ranger Battalion; 173rd Airborne Brigade; and, the multinational force in Lebanon. And from what I have observed thus far in your training you men are—and believe me it's going to cost me alot to say this—without question the most consistently best I have ever seen. If you guys perform under fire with the standards you have set here, we will all have cause to be proud. Now, here's the hard part. We will be doing some very significant and noteworthy missions. However, we can't talk to anyone about it. Our existence must be kept Top Secret. Given the nature of things, we all realize that eventually word will leak out and our existence will become known. It is imperative we delay that revelation as long as possible. Once we start, there will be a great many people looking to wax our asses. So, here's the good and bad of what you are into. You are all an integral part of the most exclusive freelance military organization in the world. You are members of the International Terrorist Suppressors Operational Force. The reaction force to combat world-wide terrorism. Your mission is to kick ass and take names—and keep your mouths shut. We all know you guys can kick ass—not bragging about it is the cobb.

"You will all be compensated equally in a manner which will deny you no creature comfort. Money will never be a problem for any of you again. We will provide you with money, cars, tropical vacations, the whole enchilada. However, we will also provide you with ultimate justice and discipline. Compromise our operation, leak intelligence or mouth off in a bar, and we'll kill you. No trial, no apologies, no appeals. Security leaks will be plugged with 240 grains from my 44 magnum Justice Duster, or one like it. Any questions?"

"Sir?" It was a young Rhodesian scout named Boris Ford.

"Yes."

"When do we get to kill something besides rattlesnakes and cockroaches?"

"How about four days from now?" as he pulled out a short black Italian Parode cigar.

His response was met by a chorus of hoots and yells—Marine grunts, screams of "Airborne," "All the Way," rebel yells, and a variety of similar exclaimations in a variety of languages.

"Sergeant Major bring up that flip chart. Hey, Willy, drop the back of that deuce and half and let's tap those kegs—these guys deserve some beer." As an easel and flip chart were set up, the bleachers emptied to the back of a truck where four beer taps started pouring into large thirty-two ounce paper cups. Everyone got a cup and moved back into the bleachers.

"Okay, settle down now. Here's the Frag Order." He proceeded to outline the situation: mission; concept of the operation; admin and logistics; command and signal. Morse finished the formal briefing, thanked the men, and said that in the morning they would polish up on some "mission oriented" training. He and Rucker left the men with the kegs of beer and a warning that training started at 0500 hours.

CHAPTER TWENTY-TWO

The Geneva meeting was billed as a seminar on international terrorism.

It consisted of a "real" program with a variety of world-wide speakers as well as several working sessions after the daily program in which the real business of I.T. was conducted. At the conclusion of the three day event there was a special question and answer session, which was closed to the press, in which Scott, Morse and the Executive Committee addressed those gathered.

"Ladies and gentlemen, thank you all for participating in our seminar. Hopefully, some of the information delivered was enlightening; perhaps even educational. However, the real purpose of our gathering is about to occur. It is imperative that everyone in this room make every concerted effort to handle this information as absolutely secret. To compromise our intentions at this stage would be disastrous. Prior to arriving you have all been subjected to both polygraph and chemical interrogation as have all of us before you. We apologize for the potential affront, and trust that you all recognize the very real need for such measures.

"I also want to thank many of you for your financial as well as moral support. We are now a very wealthy organization with the financial and human resources necessary to make an impact. And we do intend to make an impact.

"The balance of the agenda is outlined on this slide. There will be no written material disseminated during this meeting and we ask that you take no notes. I must advise you monitors will be continually scanning us to insure no one compromises the rest of us by not adhering to these conditions. I will outline the concept, direction and organization of I.T.

"The Executive Committee, comprised of Benjamin Slade, Chandler Chase, Remington Danforth, Ross W. Lasser, Byron Moore, Henry Tanaka and Ramon Gonzoles will outline the bylaws, the committee assignments and report on budget and finance. They will be followed by Colonel Jesse Morse who will submit the recommendation of guidelines for selection of targets."

Scott went on to cover his points and was followed by the others according to the agenda. After two hours and fifteen minutes of talking there was absolute silence in the room, interrupted only by the hum of the air conditioning. Then there was a growing crescendo of applause as everyone in the room rose to their feet.

The meeting was very successful. I.T. was in business.

CHAPTER TWENTY-THREE

The phone rang twice before Scott picked it up. It was the private line in his office, unknown to anyone except the Executive Committee and Colonel Morse. He had only been back home three hours since leaving the desert. He did not go on to the alternate base camp with the I.T. operational forces and staff. Instead he returned to Boston to prepare for the post mission flack.

"Hell-o?"

"Scott? Ben Slade! Some son of a bitch from Geneva talked. The word is ripping through board rooms and intelligence groups like a chain saw. The output is that a group of fascist assholes—that's us—are declaring war on terrorism. I've been dodging calls from my board of directors for hours. Chase and Danforth are dancing to the same tune."

"Calm down, Ben. It was inevitable that word would leak out. I'm just disappointed it happened so soon. We have contingency plans designed specifically for an eventuality like this. How bad can it get?"

"It depends on the individual board. With me, for example, I control about two-thirds of my board. But there is the other third that lives for the day when I step on my dick. Some of them have waited decades for a chance to throw a rock at old Benjamin Slade. They wouldn't, and couldn't, dare mess with me as long as I continue to show monster profits and pay dividends. But when they confirm that I have misappropriated corporate funds and misused the corporate trust, there will be a spontaneous group orgasm that will tilt seismographs from Maine to California. They'll concentrate on the violation of the sacred trust of the stockholders more than the money. A million bucks pissed away on R & D can easily be rationalized. But for me to participate in misdirection of those funds intentionally—they'll fucking crucify me."

"Ben—"

"Mind you, lad, we don't hold you culpable. We are all big boys. We knew what we were getting ourselves into. We still support you. But the assholes will go after our deferred compensation, stock options and any and all perks they can attack."

"Ben! Lighten up. We can handle it," said Scott as he punched into his computer terminal.

"Ingalls, you'll need Godzilla to handle this one."

"Ben, I can handle it. We knew this would happen eventually. Eventually just came a tad early. Here's what you have to do. We had planned for me to make the announcement to the media at the same time Morse concluded Floss. We may have to amend that plan. Arrange to have the Executive Committee either meet in my office in Boston tomorrow morning or link in on a conference call. We'll use the secure lines for those who can't be there in person. Ben, we can handle it. Call the rest of the Committee and reassure them. I have a few things to get moving before we meet tomorrow."

"Scott, I apologize if I'm sounding a bit frazzled. We have great trust in you, and continue to support you fully.

We believe in what we are doing, and trust you and Morse to do what is so desperately needed. It's just this is the first time we have been subjected to a potential threat we cannot control, and like most successful, powerful men, we are all selfish and used to reducing exposure."

"Ben, no apology. Get on the phone to the others. I'll see you in my office about 6 A.M."

"Good luck, pal. If I live through the night, I'll see you in the ayem."

Scott replaced the receiver and turned his attention to his computer. He punched in three dates as an access code: 9/30/17—his father's birthday; 3/22/23—his mother's birthday; and, 11/04/48—his birthday. It was his own security code; no one but him knew the sequence. Today it was the three birthdays, his father's first and his last; tomorrow would require his mother's birthday first, followed by his dad's, then his. The day after, his birthday, Mom's, then Dad's. Then the birthdays listed by day/month/year. The next sequence would be year/month/day, and so forth. Only he knew the sequence and the coding; there was no hard copy of the code. If he died, the files died with him. Morse had a similar set up with most of the files backed up on his system. "Phase Five Contingencies" appeared on the screen. Beneath it, a menu of plans. He accessed the file labeled ECC/BBC/88-004 (Executive Committee/Board Compromised/1988-Plan 004).

ECC/BDC/88-004

SITUATION: An individual or group from the Geneva meeting has compromised the existence of I.T. Knowledge of organization and missions has prompted various special interest groups to inquiry member businesses as to involvement of member companies with International Terrorist Suppressors. Result: pressure leveled against I.T. board members from their respective boards, agencies, and special interest groups.

1) Enemy Forces: SEE ANNEX
- •Situation
- •Capabilities
- •Probable courses of action

2) Friendly Forces: SEE ANNEX

MISSION: Identify who, what, why, and where threat is and eliminate.

Scott continued to review the Execution section of the plan, then typed in the coding necessary to encrypt it for dissemination to the Executive Committee.

While the computer was delivering the coded electronic mail, he poured himself three inches of Laphroig ten year old unblended scotch and deeply inhaled the peat aroma. He looked into the large mirror over his fireplace. "Here's to you, Ingalls! You have a nice face." He took a short sip of the heavy liquor and turned back to his desk and the demands of the telephone.

CHAPTER TWENTY-FOUR

Scott was in his Boylston Street office at 5:00 A.M. The first of the Executive Committee started arriving at 5:30 A.M. Chase was first, followed by Danforth, then Slade, Lasser, and the balance who came in around 5:50 A.M. As they arrived he pointed them to the sideboard set with coffee urn, mugs, plates, silver, napkins and pastry. The conference table was set with linen place mats, individual sugar and creamer sets and both water and juice filled tumblers. Additionally, there was a leather notebook at each place which contained the minutes, agendas and plans that would be discussed. At the conclusion of the meeting the documents would be shredded.

Scott broke off a discussion with Ross Lasser as the time showed 5:59 A.M. He moved to his place at the table and those who had not already sat down, did so.

"Good morning, gentlemen. Thank you for coming at such an ungodly hour."

The tension hung over the room like a mushroom cloud. He was intent on approaching his subject with a light touch.

"Can the gratuitous salutation, Ingalls, and get to the point. My sphincter is so tight it could bite off a needle," Chase snapped.

"Really, Mr. Chase! Such undignified bathroom humor from a man of your stature," said Lasser mockingly.

"My stature right now is an inch lower than whale shit, sonny," he growled.

"Knock if off, goddamn it!" Slade erupted. "Can the petty bullshit, and let Scott have his say."

A shocked silence fell over the room. These were the heavyweights of American business. They were not used to being yelled at by anyone—even someone of Benjamin Slade's stature. They also were not used to being as vulnerable and frightened as they all felt.

"Okay, guys. Let's keep calm. This security leak is really no big fucking deal. We all knew it would happen sooner or later. Well, sooner got here sooner. We are all problem solvers. Please do me the courtesy of hearing the solution to this annoyance. And gentlemen, that's all this is—an annoyance." He had their attention on several points. First, he had never before addressed them in such a manner, and he had rarely used profanity in their presence. He had always implied, or allowed to be implied his very special positioning in this power group, but he had always talked to them as a president talked to a board. Now he was talking to them like a company commander to his lieutenants. They picked up on this subtle change with mixed feelings of shock, admiration, and concern.

"You will all note that in your binders there is a detailed Operations Order for this precise eventuality. There are separate annexes for each of you detailing proposed courses of action. You will all have time this morning to review the material at length. I will summarize the concept of the operation for you and explain, in generalities, what you need to do and what you should not do. First of all, don't admit to anything. Ben has already told you all to call concurrent board meetings for tomorrow afternoon to occur at the same time as my news conference."

"Scott, that in and of itself is going to spark further questions. Many of us have directors in common. The director who gets called to an emergency Board meeting for three separate boards at the same time and day is going to be plenty suspicious," said Danforth.

"It won't matter. The point is, you are buying time until you have to face them. In the meantime, Operation Floss will be completed. In addition to the tasks outlined in your OPPLAN, I have initiated a contingency of my own."

Everyone at the table stared at him with a blend of curiosity and apprehension.

"When you meet with your boards, tell them I solicited contributions from your R & D funds to follow-up on planning suggested at the Geneva conference. Tell them you had no idea I planned to use the money in such a direct action, and that I was to submit a plan to you for the utilization of the funds next week. That will take a chunk of the heat off, if not all of it. Phase two is for you to assess what the mood of your board is. If they support the I.T. concept and the results of the Floss exercise, you're home free. If you control your board, flex your corporate muscles. Don't admit to being actively involved in the planning and control but imply you can exercise influence with this Mad Dog Ingalls."

"Scott, this is all well and good, and we all follow your reasoning. However, you are overlooking one key element," said Byron Moore as he stared into his coffee cup.

"I try not to overlook key elements. What is it, Byron?" Scott responded.

"Your own mortality. Once the word is out you are the organizer, you will be on more hit lists than George Michael. You'll be a marked man and, in short order, a dead man."

"A point well taken, Mr. Moore. However, it's handled. Last night I sold this business to a New York agency. We close tomorrow morning, six hours before I hold the press conference. One hour after the press conference, I have an appointment with a certain plastic surgeon to get a new face. Then I'm off for thirty days in a warm climate to recuperate. We will have a meeting in a month and a half so you can meet the new me. My new face will be known to only you men and Colonel Morse."

"And your plastic surgeon, and his assistants, and nurses," said Slade.

"Ben, I'm trying to insulate you men from the nitty gritty details." What he didn't want to tell the committee was the two men who would pick him up from the doctor were Kapstein and Xing. If the doctor could not be recruited to I.T., and pass the necessary loyalty tests, he would suffer a fatal accident similar to his assistants and nurses.

"Ben, I've got it covered." The man around the conference table exchanged quiet subdued glances which ended in their notebooks.

"Tell you what, lad, I won't ask the wrong questions. Then you don't have to lie."

"Ben, the problem is I won't lie to you men. We can lie to the world together, but one thing that has to be axiomatic is we don't lie to each other."

"As it should be," said Danforth.

"We appreciate your position Scott," said Chase.

"All right. Let's not get maudlin."

It was Lasser who broke the mood. "We all love and trust one another 'til death do us part."

"A poorly timed, but accurate notation, Ross," responded Moore.

"Now how about if we review the written material before us? I have to be on the West Coast for a dinner meeting."

And with that the Executive Committee of International Terrorist Suppressors continued their meeting.

CHAPTER TWENTY-FIVE

The troops were just settling into the alternate base camp and were going through the routine of cleaning equipment, checking rosters and equipment lists, reviewing mobilization plans which included load plans and all the technical stuff soldiers routinely bitched about but accomplished with the ease of breathing.

Morse had just finished writing the formal, and for real, Warning Order for Operation Floss. Despite his thirty years experience, and the fact he had written hundreds if not thousands of those suckers, he still compared his order with the format outlined in his pocket size *Ranger Handbook*, a dog-eared volume which he had memorized yet still carried. It was covered with tan card stock, the front showing the Fort Benning patch of a bayonet in a shield with the motto "*Follow Me*." Beneath and centered it was stamped *Ranger Handbook*. There was the mandatory picture of the World War Two infantryman beckoning his comrades to follow him into battle. At the bottom of the cover were three lines: *United States Army Infantry School, Fort Benning, Georgia, August 1970*. He reread from the handbook:

Part one—THE WARNING ORDER

1. General: The warning order is to warn the patrol

members of an impending mission and to organize their preparation for this mission. The format outlined below covers the information necessary for a warning order.

The detail covered in such section is determined by the patrol leader to insure proper coverage.

2. FORMAT

1. SITUATION:

   Brief statement of enemy and friendly situation.

2. MISSION:

   State in a clear concise manner and tone. Tailor to fit the patrol; however, keep it as close to the mission given in the briefing as possible.

3. GENERAL INSTRUCTIONS

   a. General and special organization to include element and team organization and individual duties.

   b. Uniform and equipment common to all, to include identification and camouflage measures.

   c. Weapons, ammunition and equipment each member will carry. Instructions for obtaining rations, water, weapons, ammunition and equipment.

   d. Chain of Command.

   e. A time schedule for the patrols guidance. Organize to show When, Where, What and Who. Also, state who will accompany patrol leader on reconnaissance. Who will supervise patrol members preparation during the patrol leaders absence. Also, special tasks for other patrol members to perform.

   f. Time, place, uniform and equipment for receiving the patrol order.

   g. Times and places for inspections and rehearsals.

4. SPECIAL INSTRUCTIONS:

a. To subordinate leaders
b. To special purpose teams or key individual.

Morse ran down his Warning Order and compared it to the Handbook outline. He smiled. When Major Robert Rogers commanded one of the first Ranger units back in 1756, he had nineteen standing orders. The first one was "Don't forget nothing." Morse pondered that order and said to himself, not withstanding the double negative, "I'll try not to, Major."

Colonel Morse issued his Warning Order to the team leaders and flight commanders. They appeared to be casually gathered around a sand table used for the briefing, but the tension that charged the air was almost tangible.

"I'll issue the Operations Order in six hours at 1200 hours. Plan on a rehearsal tonight at 2000 hours. We'll debrief on the plane en route to the assembly area. Dismissed!"

CHAPTER TWENTY-SIX

"Okay, boys and girls." Colonel Morse stood at the podium for the final briefing prior to the I.T. Operational Force departing for Libya. "We have rehearsed, briefed, briefed back, rehearsed and trained for this operation for months. It will be the first of many, and as such must be executed as flawlessly as possible. You are the very best there is in the world today. There is no doubt in my military mind on that count. You have been provided with the tools, the training and the leadership necessary to make this operation successful. Each and every one of you knows what your job is. My final order to you is very simple—Do it! If it moves, kill it. If it's stationary, blow it up. If it's portable, take it. When you guys get back, we are going to have one hellacious party. Wine, women and sunshine courtesy of International Terrorist Suppressors. That's all."

As he stepped down from the podium he was greeted with a spontaneous grunting yell delivered in unison by over 250 of the worlds best fighting men as they rose to their feet and assumed the position of attention.

"H-E-E-E-Y-A-A-A-A-W-W-H-H-H-H!"

Morse walked slowly down the center aisle of the briefing room to the back where Scott was seated. When he reached the back of the room he smiled at Scott and said, "Here we go, sport. When those guys get through with that camp, every news gathering organization in the free world won't know whether to shit, piss or go blind."

"Colonel, as long as they don't go deaf and dumb on us, I'll be happy."

"You're in the third aircraft with me. Let's go do it."

The I.T. Operational Force departed from the training site on a dog-legged route which included a stop in an isolated New Hampshire location before departing for the next checkpoint over Greenland; then England to refuel; and, onto the Assembly Area in the southwest of Egypt. Everyone disembarked from the aircraft for a pit stop and to stretch their legs while Colonel Morse and Scott went to meet with Kapstein to review the final Blackbird photos of the target.

"So, Jer, how does it look?" asked Morse.

"Everything's a go, Colonel. The Russian visitors are apparently on site, about 200 or so from the number of vehicles and foot traffic. The 105's are here for the diversionary force, and Sid added some Willy Peter (white phosphorus) rounds to add to the confusion."

"Okay, I'm gonna have the troops crash for a rest before we cross the LD. Have the section heads and team commanders report to my CP for a final final."

"Yes, sir!" snapped the G-2.

Morse turned to Ingalls and grinned.

"Well, son, here we are down to the short strokes. How does it feel?"

"I'd be lying if I said I wasn't nervous as a whore in church."

"Goes with the territory sport."

The final briefing was short and to the point. Morse ran

down the Op order stanza and verse and there were no questions. The troops would get a four hour nap and mount the aircraft for the actual assault. Local mercenaries provided perimeter security, not knowing who they were guarding, why, or what this formidable group was about to do.

Meanwhile, several thousand miles away, an unsuspecting Russian Light Colonel and a Libyan base commander were drinking vodka. Across an ocean, in the District of Columbia, a freshman U.S. Senator was chairing a meeting to investigate an old college chum; and, in the Harvard Club on Boston's Commonwealth Avenue Ben Slade and a group of visiting businessmen were drinking Remy Martin Cognac, smoking cigars and pausing frequently to look at their watches.

CHAPTER TWENTY-SEVEN

While the subordinate commanders were briefing their people, Morse settled into a cup of coffee and a cigar in the Command Post. Everything was going smoothly—the way it ought to.

"Got a minute, boss?" It was Jerry Kapstein smiling his way into the Colonel's quiet time.

"I always have time for my G-2 and my boss—in that order, too." He smiled as he pulled a stool up for Kapstein to sit on.

"We just received some new intelligence, Colonel, and it's rather nice."

"You gonna make me beg, or are you playing it for drama?"

"Sorry, skipper. Here it is: good news first; then the bad news. The good news is we have learned that the Russians are sending a large shipment of VX gas and some fancy new nerve rucker-upper to our target for tests and storage. Also, there will be a top top *top* secret delivery of some new biological beast that makes the Andromeda Strain look like postnasal drip."

"All right, that's good news. We can neutralize more stuff and pinch the Red Bear's butt in the process. What's the bad news?" he asked.

"We'll need to delay the assault for four days."

"That's okay. It will be a pain in the ass for the 4, and you. You'll both need to reschedule all the logistical stuff, but it should be more than worth it."

"Normally, I'd agree sir, but I just talked to Scott, and he's got some board problems. His solution is linked to our assault going off on time as scheduled."

"That's his problem, and our deal. Politics will not impede tactical operations."

"Yes, sir! But we'll need to find a way to keep him alive for the extra four days. Otherwise, he'll be meeting Jimmy Hoffa."

"Captain, perhaps you had best give me all the details."

Kapstein reiterated the story of Ingalls and the Executive Committee.

Morse picked up the telephone and called Ingalls.

"Scott Ingalls' residence." It was the voice of a cultured and confident woman, certainly no maid.

"Leslie, is that you?"

"Who's asking?" The politeness went out of her voice.

"It's Jesse Morse. Is Scott home?"

"I'll get him. He's in the den, and he looks like shit."

"Hey, sport. Your lady says you look like shit. Can you talk?"

"Yeah, this is a secure line. I take it Jerry told you of my little timing problem?"

"I got ya covered, bossman. How's about you and Ben meeting me at O'Hare for breakfast tomorrow morn?"

"Let's make it lunch. Ben's twice my age, and the schedule we've been running is smoking my butt."

"I'll see you in the coffee shop next to the United check-in."

"Handled!" Scott hung up the phone as Leslie came up behind him and started kneading his shoulders.

"Les, things are about to get complicated, and a lot of it I can't share with you just yet. How would you like to go away for a month and do nothing but sit in the sun, swim and make love?"

"Does Howdy Doody have a wooden ass?"

"Be ready to leave in four days. I need to go to Chicago tomorrow and from there I have a couple of other stops. I'll pick you up in four days at the Newport place."

"I can't wait. Where are we going anyway?"

"It's a secret."

"Okay, boss. It doesn't matter anyhow. What's in Chicago?"

"Lunch." With that he went back into his den and his computer.

Scott was ticking away at his computer when Leslie walked into the room. He turned and looked at her over his shoulders.

"I'll be right with you, babe," he said.

"Take your time . . . I'll make us a couple of Nigronis."

"Ah. Equality for Campari, Cinzano and vodka. What was it Jean Paul called them?"

"Efficient."

"Yeah. That's appropriate." He turned back to his computer, punched a series of buttons and the printer kicked on. With the printer clacking away, he got up and walked up behind Leslie as she was making the drinks.

"Okay, work's done. What should I get into now?"

"How about me?" she said with an alluring half smile.

"Works for me!" He turned her around, holding her close and kissed her deeply. The phone rang and he broke the contact.

"Ingalls, you have just been saved by the bell," said Leslie as she returned to making the drinks.

"That's just the first round. I intend to take the phone off the hook before round two begins." He picked up the telephone.

"Scott Ingalls speaking."

"Howdy, Scott. Hope I didn't interrupt anything?" asked Colonel Morse.

"Not yet . . . another five minutes would have been interrupting. What's up?"

"We're all set for Chicago. I'm beginning to feel like a chairborne logistics type rather than an old ground pounder."

"Colonel, before we're through you'll qualify for a seat on the Joint Chiefs."

"Heaven forbid!"

"I can't speak for heaven, but I'm sure everyone else in the Defense Department will forbid it—forever. You might even get screwed out of your pension."

"Scott me lad—no guts no glory—I don't want no stinking pension anyway."

"Okay . . . I'll meet you in the coffee shop in Chicago. Have Ben link up with us there."

"Wilco!"

"Now if you'll forgive me, I have some linking up of my own to do right now."

"Give the lady my best."

"Actually, I planned on giving her my best. Ingalls out."

CHAPTER TWENTY-EIGHT

When Scott and Ben joined Morse outside the coffee shop they looked like three stages of physical condition. Morse was tall, fit and his white hair contrasted with his sun-baked skin and steel grey eyes yielding a result that was nothing if not totally impressive. Not a stewardess or woman between eight and eighty saw him without staring. A few even grew so bold as to extend offers. Scott was in the middle. He was handsome and well groomed but lacked the charismatic ambiance enjoyed by Morse. Ben Slade looked like a before ad for a health farm. He was bald, overweight, his skin a pasty white, and he had baggy brown pouches under his eyes. Despite all that, he had eyes that commanded respect and warned anyone who looked into them "don't fuck with me."

"I've got a plan for your problem, Scott," said Morse.

"So have I," he responded.

"Tell you what. You show me yours and I'll show you mine." The colonel led his two co-conspirators off to a booth in the corner of the coffee shop.

Both plans were remarkably similar except for a pivotal element. Scott had planned to tape the announcement on video, have his surgery and boogie south leaving release of the tape to his Executive Committee.

Morse nixed that plan for simple reasons. "Suppose the assault ends up being different than we project? How can you announce bad guy body count until we kill 'em. How can you report what is actually in the camp, until we get there? We just learned of this new shipment. What if there is other stuff there we don't know of yet? One of the key ingredients to your news conference has to be reporting the combat intelligence we gather on the ground. And you simply cannot do that until we do our number."

"You're right on all counts, Colonel—as usual. What do you propose?" asked Scott.

"And don't forget that the buzzing going on frequently mentions our boy wonder here. There's a real chance that there may already be a contract out on blue eyes here." Ben Slade looked around the coffee shop.

"Benjamin, Scott, the new implied task to this mission is simply stated, 'to keep Scott Ingalls alive' long enough for him to deliver his message to the world press, and have his face changed. The best way to do that is obvious. Scott returns south with me to the base camp. He stays in isolation with us until we are done and debriefed. He can make his announcement from a studio Lasser has provided us and I'll have a special I.T. security team escort him to the doctors, and then to his R & R site. Scotty, you did your end of this deal superbly. You packaged the concept, put the players together and collected the money. You once said that you would do your job, and leave me the freedom to do mine. Well, sport, keeping you alive to fight another day is part of my job, and I do my job very well."

"The Colonel is right, son. The safest place for you is in the middle of your own private army. Although we regret the timing is poor, we can survive. You can count on your Executive Committee serving you up as Judas goat to our respective boards. Although candidly, I think with few exceptions, most of the boards will eventually fall in line. For those that don't, well we have been the sad victims of the nefarious Scott Ingalls." Ben delivered his message over the brim of an ironstone coffee mug.

"Okay, you guys win. It makes all the sense in the world. I suppose the Department of the Army will take away my commission, huh Colonel?" He grinned like a child.

"Count on it, sport. You'll lose your USAR Majority quicker than a minnow can swim a dipper. So what? You're already a goddamn General."

Scott and the Colonel said good-bye to Slade at the United security check station. Scott didn't refund his ticket, instead he gave it to a young college man with a tennis racket.

"Okay, Colonel, do what you do best—lead on."

"This way, boss. We have a private jet waiting for us over yonder."

They walked out to the holding area for private planes and he saw Victor Cachon in the cockpit of a Lear Fantail jet.

CHAPTER TWENTY-NINE

The scene Ben Slade was suffering through was being repeated in numerous board rooms elsewhere across the country. It placed him in a situation he was unfamiliar with and certainly didn't enjoy—being vulnerable.

He was right when he had told Scott that he had enemies who had literally waited decades for an opportunity like this to attack his power base. And they were certainly enjoying the opportunity to throw rocks and challenge his position.

"You mean to sit there and tell us that you actually paid this Ingalls fellow one million dollars before he provided a specific program of work as to how the money would be utilized?" Jonathan Winters was delivering the harange. He was an investment banker from Boston's North Shore. He lived in the exclusive town of Wenham only five miles from the son of General George Patton. The son was a General too (Major General, two stars, retired). Winters was very Harvard, a major stockholder, who had hated Slade's guts for more reasons than Carter had pills. The most dominate reason was the most simple to understand—jealousy. He viewed this situation as a major opportunity to discredit Slade, and maybe (hope upon hope) even get him fired.

"That's right, Jon." Ben was trying very hard to remain calm although his ulcers were blazing.

"Ben, speaking as a major stockholder in the company, I find it most disturbing that the man charged with the control of our best interest could make such a bumbling error. I mean, this Ingalls fellow dropped out of the MBA program at Harvard. He's in advertising, for Christ's sake. What the hell ever possessed you to trust him, let alone give him a million dollars of our stockholders money? Mr. Slade, I feel that you have sorely misused the trust of this corporation, and failed miserably in protecting the interest of this company. This sort of tacit support for what can only be termed a mercenary organization of terrorists can turn into a cancer which can ultimately impact on our position in the marketplace and erode profits."

That was the trump card, and despite his resolve, Ben responded.

"Fuck you, Jon! How dare you take that tone with me. I'm not one of your MBA students dedicated to your hubris and browbeatings. You were not with us in Geneva. Ingalls raised some very salient issues at their conference, and he succeeded in convincing not only me, but a large group of my peers that he could offer solutions to problems and make a profit for our shareholders. I shouldn't have to, but I will also remind you that it has been Benjamin Slade who took this cesspool of inefficiency, embarrassing market share and routine losses to the point where we now dominate our competition and routinely pay handsome dividends to our stockholders. That is the job I have done, and I have done it better than anyone else in the history of our industry. If you don't believe me read the *Wall Street Journal, Business Week, Fortune, Forbes* and *The Economist*. Your big Brahmin mouth is dangerously close to writing a check your body can't cash."

"Now see here, Benjamin . . ."

"Gentlemen, gentlemen . . " Joe DelSesto spoke up calming things down. He was a short barrel-chested steelman from Philadelphia. He also was a major stockholder, and a wildcard in that his support in the past had gone to both Slade and Winters, depending on the issue. He could, and had been the deciding swing vote in other controversies.

"Ben, no one is challenging your past accomplishments, or your intentions. I assure you that we all have great confidence and respect for your ability. No one here would ever suggest that your value to the corporation has been diminished by this unfortunate incident. Would we Jonathan?" He looked directly into the face of Winters, who averted his gaze. "The last thing any of us wants to do is piss you off to the point where you accept any of those myriad offers our competition tries to tempt you with. You turned this company around almost single-handedly, and if others choose to forget that, I certainly cannot." There were nods of agreement around the table. Winters was turning the color of an overripe beet.

"All we want to know, Ben, is how bad can we be hurt by this? No one here would ever suggest that you wildcatted on us and funded this I.T. thing unilaterally knowing how Ingalls was going to use the money. Our concerns are more PR-oriented. You have made us hundreds of times the amount paid, and hopefully will continue to do so. But we need to know where do we go from here?"

"Joe, I'm as upset by this as all of you. I apologize for the outburst, but it offends me to see Jonathan being such a shit. The good and bad of this situation is complex. We can't get hurt competitively because candidly, our competitors also participated. Money was apparently provided by Detroit, New York, Hollywood, Atlanta, Dallas, and virtually every significant *Fortune 500* company. Actually, if

Ingalls is successful, we all stand to benefit from what he's doing, although none of us may condone his methods. The man took advantage of all of us, and misused a trust. He had his own hidden agenda with which he was proceeding. However, I feel we are in a position to benefit from the best of both worlds. We should openly condemn the man as a con man and a terrorist in his own right. But we should in the privacy of our own prayers hope that he is successful in what he does, because we benefit from his program. We cannot ever appear to agree with his methods but I for one wish him success. The guy is good. He not only duped me, but apparently some 400 others, and that gentlemen is no mean feat."

"I still say you get screwed, Ben." It was Winters again.

"And we don't pay you the big bucks to see you get screwed by some snot nose dropout."

"Jonathan! Sure, Ingalls may have duped me, but he didn't screw me or this corporation. However, there are two points to consider: first, if he succeeds in his efforts, at least I get a kiss; and secondly, he didn't get any cherry." Everyone in the room started to laugh—it broke the tension. ". . . and as for Ingalls being some snot nose dropout, you may note that the man has made a career of being successful. He was a top student at Brown University as well as a top athlete, both college and AAU. He was a star at Harvard before he walked away from the MBA program, perhaps his greatest plus. He finished in the top of virtually every military school he went through and he went through the toughest: Airborne; Ranger; Pathfinder; Special Forces. He distinguished himself in two combat tours in Vietnam which yielded a Distinguished Service Cross, Two Silver Stars, Three Bronze Stars, a

Purple Heart and gaggle of other doodads to include the Vietnamese Medal of Gallantry. He came back to break into the highly competitive New York advertising arena, and excelled there before starting his own business in Boston with a couple of grand and an old Underwood typewriters. According to my staff, he just sold his business today for eleven million dollars. Hardly the sort of individual I'd call a snot nose dropout, Mr. Winters."

"You sound like you want to hire the son of a bitch," said Winters.

"If I could, I sure as hell would."

"Hey, fellas." It was one of the until then silent board members who spoke up. "How about we get our high-priced PR honcho on the horn and outline the problem so we can start protecting our position in this mess, rather than spend the whole day bitching at one another?"

"An excellent idea! Pass the coffee, please," said another one of the silent tycoons.

"Joe, could I see you for a minute in my office?" asked Slade.

As DelSesto and Slade walked out of the conference room, Winters sat fuming.

As he closed the door, Slade turned to DelSesto and said: "Joe, we've had our differences in the past, but I want you to know that I appreciate your support in there."

"Save your thanks, Ben, and don't you ever do that again." There was an awkward pause as DelSesto glowered at Ben.

"I beg your pardon?" Slade responded with a confused look.

"Ben, you don't know how to beg. Come on, don't insult our intelligence. There isn't a man in that room that doesn't believe you did precisely what we all deny. You misused that money and scapegoated Ingalls, probably with his knowledge. I stepped in to prevent Winters from demanding your resignation for a couple of reasons—none of them linked to any great affection for you. First, you are the best, and the company would suffer greatly from your loss, or worse, from your defection to the competition. I was protecting our assets, and you, despite your many sins of hubris, are a key asset. Secondly, I think you are basically well intended in what you did, if not incredibly myopic. If your friend Ingalls can make an impact, it certainly would help, and a million bucks is a cheap buy in."

"Joe . . ."

"Shut up. I'm not done yet. If you had used even half that money for your own personal benefit we would have nailed you: both in the Boardroom and in the press. However, you apparently did what you have done so skillfully in the past—you made an end run around us. You tend to do that when you think you are right and we might not approve or support you. So far, you have usually been right. I hope you're right this time. Because Ben, although we permit you to more or less have your head, there are limits. Fuck up and we'll hand you your head. Today you came dangerously close to those limits. If this thing blows up and taints us in a way so as to erode profits or endanger our market position, I'll send my cousin Louie from Federal Hill in Providence to visit you. Then I'll read a glowing eulogy at your funeral. Have I made myself clear?"

"Sufficiently."

"Okay, now let's go back and join the rest. And look happy, it will piss off Winters no end."

CHAPTER THIRTY

Scott sat in the back of the briefing room while Morse issued the Operations Order, and answered questions from the team leaders. Some hours later he would again sit in the back of the room when the section and team leaders would go up to the podium to issue the brief back. Later, he remembered with considerable clarity the detail and enthusiasm with which each man spoke to his teams or sections about their duties and responsibilities.

All was in readiness when the hour of departure approached. Jerry Kapstein had an NCO monitoring press activity. The G-2 section had a bank of wire machines which were ticking off the latest news from Associated Press, United Press International, and Reuters. Additionally, there was one person per shift assigned to monitor the news on the Cable News Network. All these sources reported almost simultaneously the world-wide search for Scott Ingalls. He was identified as a Boston advertising executive who reportedly was attempting to organize some sort of nebulous terrorist organization. He reportedly had bilked hundreds of businessmen world-wide out of millions of dollars under false pretenses and was considered to be both armed and dangerous. Any information leading to his capture would be rewarded from a fund established by the involved businesses.

Kapstein reported all the information to Colonel Morse.

As the troops gathered in the assembly area in preparation for departure, Kapstein received his last satellite pictures of the target site. Although it was noted there was increased traffic into the facility, there were significant changes. The last bit of intelligence (a Blackbird flyover) would arrive about an hour and a half prior to the assault force crossing the line of departure.

Morse was experiencing that adrenaline induced rush which he had secretly admitted to himself years ago was his narcotic.

CHAPTER THIRTY-ONE

Meanwhile, several thousand miles away, Major Amad Hussen, commander of the terrorist training camp was greeting Lieutenant Colonel Vladimir Petrovich, Commander of a Russian Airborne Battalion.

"Welcome to the nest of the desert spider comrade," said Hussen.

"Thank you, Major. Let us get the shipments put to bed and then discuss security, if you please." Petrovich was ramrod straight and very proper. He resembled a character out of Chekhov more than a field commander of the Union of Soviet Socialist Republics.

"Yes, sir!" barked Hussen. He was both anxious to show off his facility to this Russian benefactor and nervous not to overlook any minor detail which might be reported to his superiors.

After the gases and biological agents had been secured, the two officers met in Amad's office.

"May I offer you some refreshment, Colonel?" asked the Major, reaching for a bottle of chilled Stolichnaya vodka.

"Thank you, Major. I see despite the song of the desert you still have some of life's necessities." He was smiling as he reached for the vodka that was being poured.

"When a man deals in the currency of death, it becomes more necessary to live life to the fullest comrade." The two men toasted.

"How is your security, Major?" asked Petrovich, pouring himself another vodka.

"The best! We have seismic intrusion devices around the perimeter and the avenues of approach. Our physical security includes both passive and active devices. We rotate shifts every three hours to guarantee maximum alertness. Building TA 3555 cannot be entered without prior clearance. No person is ever admitted to the building without being accompanied by one of the technicians, myself included. The chemicals and biological agents are all stored in the second basement of the building in climate controlled storage bins, depending on the requirements of the chemical and its temperature balance. The provisions for TA 3255—the Communications building—are similar except that an authorized individual may enter unaccompanied. All air in-let and out-take vents are manned by armed guards. All incoming visitors, such as you and your men, are isolated from the operational elements of the camp until fingerprint checks are verified—as they have been for you and your group sir. Additionally, we have the capability of jamming all known NATO and WARSAW PACT electronic equipment. Finally, very few people even know of our existence. Your gas and virus are safe and secure here, comrade."

"Very good, Major."

Hussen literally beamed like a young schoolboy bathed in the glow of a superior's approval.

"However, until the virus is dispatched, please increase your already commendable precautions," Petrovich said while extracting one of the potent cardboard and paper tubes euphemistically called cigarettes by the Russians.

Hussen's smile and glow vanished as if his light switch has just been flicked. "Yes, sir!" was his immediate response. Followed by concern and confusion. "Have I not adequately provided for security, my Colonel?" he asked.

"Yes, yes, Major, your security is superior. I ask only that you increase your already superior level and measures one step higher."

"As you order, sir." However, Hussen was secretly concerned. He had already shortened this shifts from four hours to three to impress this Russian. To do so had cut deeply into his duty roster. Stretching the resources further would no doubt increase dissension already precipitated by long tours in the remote desert outpost, not to mention hard physical and mental work without the benefit of family or women. Both his students and faculty were becoming sloppy and showing signs of lost motivation. "Comrade, if you will excuse me, I will make the necessary arrangements before evening prayer. Then I must join my brothers in Islam at prayer. Please make yourself at home. If you require anything, just ask Rashid. He will see to your wants." Major Amad Hussen left his Russian visitor. He was thinking about the Russian finishing off the expensive vodka which had cost him the staggering sum of forty-five U.S. dollars for the liter.

CHAPTER THIRTY-TWO

"Well, Jer, what do you think?" asked Colonel Morse.

"Colonel, this plan offers all the best elements of Kampala, Son Tay, and the Yom Kippur Ambush. In fact, it's kind of poetic from a Jew's point of view. We should hit them just as they begin their morning prayers. We should catch those Libyan sodomites with their dirty asses in the air and their heads buried in their prayer rugs."

"Don't get ethnic on me, Kapstein. Don't forget there will probably be a couple of hundred Soviet types who won't have their faces buried in the sand. The original plan had not counted on them."

"Ah-h-h, Colonel, there are two sides to that sword, and each one is equally sharp," interrupted Xing. "There are more defenders, but they occupy the same space. Therefore, they are tactically inefficient. Our kill is doubled with the Russians also. Additionally, we have added the extra 105mm section to the diversionary force. Once they land, they will immediately fire a full battery into the center of the camp for effect. The last round should hit seconds before the helicopters take out the towers. Captain

Long's team will have to be extra careful not to slip in the resulting blood and guts which will cover the ground."

"We'll be cutting it rather close though, Colonel." said Morse gravely.

"Colonel, in the words of Mr. Ingalls—'No guts, no glory.' " The small Vietnamese smiled as he realized the bad pun.

CHAPTER THIRTY-THREE

The subcommittee of the Senate Intelligence Committee was chaired by Calvin Pastor. This assignment was both a blessing and a curse: an uncommon appointment for a junior Senator but risky because of his acknowledged association with Scott Ingalls. The speculation about his appointment was as varied as it was pervasive. One school of Washington pundits claimed he got the appointment because of his old man, the former Speaker of the House, either was a plum to acknowledge the Speakers past support or as a poisoned apple for the Speakers past arrogance. Another segment of Monday morning speculators claimed it was because Calvin had gone to school with Ingalls and could better control the direction of the inquiry than any other. A third, more cynical faction, contended Pastor got the assignment because no one else wanted it. The truth was a combination, plus he had asked for it.

"Gentlemen, as I see it, we need to do several things. First, we must locate this Scott Ingalls. Concurrently, we should contact all those who attended his so-called seminar on terrorism in Geneva. The focus of our investigation should strive to determine what his actual intentions are, what specific laws may have been broken, how much actual funding this group has and what their immediate intentions might be," recited Senator Pastor.

"Senator, as I understand it, you know this man and he actually told you of his plan," said the senior Senator from Connecticut.

"Yes and no, Senator. I know Scott. We went to Harvard together and have been casual acquaintances since then. He did outline his idea for this I.T. thing, but he claimed it was a movie script for a client. It is precisely because of my past friendship with the man and the manner in which he attempted to use me that I have called this meeting. For whatever ill placed sense of purpose he may embrace, the man's grasp exceeds his reach. He has crossed the one line no man can be allowed to cross and that is the line of the law."

"As I see it Senator, you are fanning a dead fire," said the Senator from Kentucky. "This is a simple case of fraud. He bilked a group of greedy big business types out of a chunk of money and that's it. It's a case for Justice, not a Senate committee. Granted, such a committee could be a sweet plum for an ambitious freshman Senator with an influential family, but I, for one, am somewhat reticent to launch, or be associated with a Red Herring. If this is just a finesse by you to cover your errors in judgment, I find the entire affair beneath the dignity of the Senate."

"Senator, I'll not deny that my knowing Ingalls is a political embarrassment. However, for you to suggest that an investigation into the activities of a bright, wealthy, and highly decorated former Green Beret with designs on conducting paramilitary actions on foreign soil, potentially in the name of democracy and free enterprise, is beneath our dignity, I suggest you are sorely myopic."

"Now see here, young man . . ." responded the senior man.

"Don't 'young man' me, Senator. Neither do I care to hear about how my father would never approve. The Speaker has counseled me on this matter, and he and I are in total agreement that this Ingalls issue does require our attention. The man needs to be stopped before he can do any real harm. What if he succeeds in doing something foolish."

"That is unlikely, Senator," said the Connecticut Senator.

"It is very likely, Senator. I might remind the venerable Senator from Kentucky that Israel was successful with their Entebbe raid, even if we failed with Iran. Ross Perot, another civilian, launched a freelance thrust into Teheran to rescue some of his executives and he was successful. Scott is very intelligent, apparently has the resources, the experience and the connections to duplicate the Perot feat elsewhere. Gentlemen we are on very shaky ground. If we condemn him as an outlaw and he succeeds where we, through normal diplomatic channels have failed, the credibility of the United States—which is already on tenuous ground for being all bark and no bite—could be in real jeopardy. The last thing we need at this point, with the mideast as volatile as tinder and Africa in turmoil, is to have freelancers doing what we should be able to handle as a nation. We cannot publicly condemn him because of the potential for public support rallying to his cause. And we cannot condone his activities because they are ipso facto illegal. I have called this meeting not in an attempt to cover my political or public image tail, but to solicit the advice and counsel of men more experienced than I, whose opinions I value and respect."

That last bit was a nice touch, he thought. Strike for the ego and the hearts and minds will follow.

"Very well, Calvin, go on," said the Senator from Connecticut with a slight half smile on his face.

CHAPTER THIRTY-FOUR

The plan was for Colonel Morse and the staff to establish an Operational Control Base in the southern desert of Egypt and monitor the progress of the assault. Morse insisted that on this first mission he accompany the assault team onto the ground. Sid Bullerwell would be in charge of the Command Post and would manage the message flow and logistics. A reserve force of two platoons—about eighty-four men—would remain behind with the staff to provide security and be available in case of an unanticipated "what if."

Little did Bullerwell or the reserve know that they would be more than routinely busy in the next forty-eight hours.

The troops marshaled at the landing zone and were going through their final inspections as Morse walked up to Ingalls on the runway.

"Well, sport. Here goes!"

"Colonel, I have to admit I'm a bit jealous."

"Come on, Scott, I thought that ass whipping Xing gave you convinced you to stay behind the desk."

"My mind knows I'm assuming the right role, but my gut is tickled with adrenaline and pride over what you guys are going into."

"God forgive us all, but there's nothin' like the smell of

cordite in the heat of battle to turn on an old war horse like me.''

''I know what you mean, and that's why I'm jealous. Bring 'em all back, Colonel.''

''You got it, pal.'' The two men shook hands, parting with a final slap on the shoulder.

''Don't forget . . .'' Scott started to say, ''. . . to kick ass and take names,'' finished Morse with a big smile.

As Scott watched the larger than life Morse mount the CH-47-C Chinook helicopter, Bullerwell walked up behind him.

''Mr. Ingalls, this is without question the best planned raid I have ever had the pleasure to be associated with. The Ground Tactical Plan, Intelligence, Landing, Air Movement, Supporting Plan, Operations Requirements, Logistics Requirements, and even the Debriefing Outline are all letter perfect. We've thought of every contingency conceivable except Armageddon. We should release the written material to friendly military schools for inclusion in future training programs.''

''Sid, all we did was homogenize all that stuff from all the best schools and add a few lessons learned from our collective experience. We didn't write any new books on this one, we just fine tuned the basics already being employed by the most conventional forces.''

''Beggin' your pardon, sir, but to characterize the I.T. force as anywhere near conventional is, I'm afraid, a gross distortion.''

''Well, maybe you're right, Major. But you know as well as I that if we spent another year adding contingencies, there would be that one wrinkle—a sun spot, or a coup, or an earthquake—that could never be anticipated that could fuck up even the most perfectly planned operation.''

''Sir, unless the Soviet bloc decides to conduct war games in that compound within the next hour, the only outcome to the exercise is going to be a very hot charred chunk of sand in the desert.''

''I hope you're right, Sid.''

''How about a nice cup of tea, sir?''

''Sidney, unless it's made with Colombian coffee beans, I doubt there is such a thing as a nice cup of tea.''

''Oh, Mister Ingalls, how can a man so right be so wrong?''

''Come on, Major, I'll watch you drink a cup of tea.''

''Right you are, sir.'' As the first element of the I.T. air movement took off, Scott and Bullerwell walked to the CP tent.

They were met at the entrance to the tent by Captain Bobbie Jones, a non-neck ex-marine with a faded *Semper Fi* tattoo on his forearm. ''Major, we just picked up something you might find interesting.''

''Warsaw Pact war games in Libya?'' he asked with a half smile.

''No, sir. Another hijacking.''

''Shit,'' said Scott. ''Who, what, when and where?'' he asked.

''I'll let the Intell Sergeant fill you men in. I need to see my Platoon Sergeant,'' and Jones ran off to the Mess tent.

''Okay, Sergeant, what have you got?'' asked the I.T. Executive Officer.

''Staff Sergeant Tucker, a tall—six feet six inches—Texan who had served in Nam with the 173rd Airborne Brigade before returning to Amarillo to discover that the cowboy's life was no longer exciting, responded: ''About forty-five minutes ago, a squad of Shiite Moslems grabbed a Pan Am jet in Athens. They immediately killed an American tourist and his wife, and cut the tongue out of an Israeli diamond merchant. They have demanded the release of fifty of their kind from camps in Israel, and one million dollars from the United States. They have said they will kill a passenger every two hours until their demands are met."

"What are the Greeks doing?" asked Scott.

"It's a bit early, sir, but the impression is, they're playing with themselves."

"Sid, get Jones back here and have him joined by Bullock, Ny, Wakefield and that Irish helicopter jockey."

"What do you have in mind, sir?"

"Sidney, we've got over eighty men here with nothing to do except listen to radio traffic and drink coffee, or tea." He added the last with a smile.

"This one is simple. We've got a dozen scenarios in the SOP for this type thing. We're going to take back that aircraft."

"Shouldn't we wait, sir?"

"He who hesitates is lost, major. We may be a lot of things, but we ain't lost. Get me my computer and a cup of real coffee."

"Yes, sir," replied Bullerwell with a look of genuine concern on his hard face.

The I.T. Operational Force was in the third and final dogleg of their movement. They were flying at 200 feet, below radar and under radio silence. Men were checking weapons and tightening tie-downs as the sound of the aircraft enveloped them in a cocoon of quietude.

Major Bullerwell stood in the Command Post tent lighting his pipe as the last of the men entered. He looked nervous. Scott looked excited. "Gents, Mr. Ingalls has a little job for you."

Scott walked up to the front of the tent and slipped back the cover on a large pad resting on an easel. "For those of you who felt left out by being assigned to the reserve—forget it. We just got another mission."

"All right!" shouted two NCO's.

"Here's the deal. Unlike the Libya assault, we don't get a bunch of rehearsals on this one. However, this may prove to become routine to us, so I expect you hard cases can pull it off and be back in time for the party."

There was a ripple of heads turning to look at one another before coming to rest on Ingalls.

"This is simple, straightforward, and SOP. I'll issue the Frag Order now. You'll have less than an hour to brief your troops, gather equipment and mount up for a move. Here's the drill." He proceeded to outline, in typical military fashion, the situation, mission, concept of the operation, specifics of execution, logistics, command and signal. The economy with which he issued the order impressed everyone, including Bullerwell. Thirty minutes later he finished with his standard close. "Gentlemen, what are your questions?"

Jones looked around him then stood up all smiles and said, "Sir, you answered all the questions, and then some. We'll see you in an hour." The reserve forces rose and left the room.

"Sir?" Bullerwell walked up to Ingalls.

"Yeah?"

"You rattled that off like you expected this to happen. That was the most complete Frag Order I have ever heard. Can we really do it?"

"Fucking A we can do it. And Sid, I did expect it. Oh, not this one, and not now. But eventually, somewhere, sometime. This is the most common type of terrorist attack next to bombings and assassinations. This plan is the most effective way to handle it. We won't always use this plan but, for today, given the surprise target of opportunity, it's the odds on favorite."

"Somehow, I just didn't expect us to lose our virginity to two missions at the same time."

"Neither did I, major. Ain't it a bitch."

"This will leave us with only forty men here, sir."

"No problem, Sid. That's twice the coffee and tea for those who remain."

"Yes, sir. I never thought of that."

CHAPTER THIRTY-FIVE

Before Senator Pastor recessed his committee meeting, there were two I.T. strike forces in the air. The Libyan company lead by Colonel morse was just ten minutes from dropping the diversionary force, and Captain Jones' team was just taking off for Athens.

The diversionary force hit the ground and moved only about a mile before they set the battery. The computer quickly plotted the coordinates for the fire effect. Meanwhile, in the camp the early warning devices were picking up activity on the desert floor to the south east. Hussen had just entered the communications shed to confer with his section leader when the Russians walked in behind him.

"What is it, my friend? Lost camels?"

"I'm not sure, comrade. Based on the metal detector readings and the seismic reports, it appears to be a heavily reinforced platoon."

"Are you expecting anyone other than me?"

"No sir, my Colonel. It just appeared out of nowhere. That would suggest an airdrop."

"I'll call my troops."

"No, sir, that won't be necessary. I'll send a platoon out

to intercept them. You weren't expecting any more troops, were you, sir?''

''No, no. And if more were to come, they would land right here in the camp. I don't like this, Major Hussen.''

''It may be some kind of drill. But I don't think so. We'll know soon enough. Sergeant, muster the mechanized platoon for immediate reaction drill.''

''What can I do to help?'' asked the Russian.

''It is nothing, I'm sure, but perhaps for the form of the drill, you could arm your men and have them establish a perimeter around the center two buildings.''

''I will return shortly.''

''Abdullah, what could it be?''

''By the Prophet, Major, I can't be sure.''

After dropping the diversionary force, Morse moved the balance of the force toward the Objective Rallying Point and had the various elements break off. The assault elements were slowly moving toward their final checkpoints as the terrorist reactionary force left the camp heading southeast at about thirty miles an hour. When they had gone almost half way toward the I.T. ground element, the computers had triangulated the compound and the guns were set.

Since timing and surprise were essential, they fired four rounds: one short, one long, one left and one right and finished with a fire for effect on the center of the triangulation.

Petrovich had just finished positioning his men around the two center buildings when he heard the familiar and frightening sound of incoming. He rushed to the Communications shed but was unable to get in the locked door. As he pounded on the door for entrance, a 105mm howitzer shell landed twenty feet behind him showering him with shards of shrapnel which shredded his body and literally tore his head from his shoulders. The artillery was leaving a frothy wake of torn bodies, equipment and buildings. Of the 200 some Russian troops who were standing at parade rest around the buildings, only twelve survived the initial fire for effect and three of those are bleeding to death trying to stuff their intestines back into their torn abdomens.

Hussen was in a panic. He knew this was no drill, but he couldn't imagine who would attack them. This camp was a top secret training facility nestled in the ultimate protection of Colonel Khadaffi's bosom.

As suddenly as it started, the barrage stopped. The silence was punctuated by the screaming and soft moaning of dying men. As the dust started to settle, the cadre and students of the base came cautiously out of their buildings. Some were armed, some were not. They were in an assortment of undress and obviously both confused and frightened. They had been indoctrinated with the belief that they were the wolves who attacked and destroyed. They were not prepared to be defenders. As they choked on the dust and tried to clear their eyes of the carnage, they were again surprised as they heard monstrous explosions. Those who looked up saw the guard towers erupting in huge fireballs. 20mm cannon and flachette rounds riddled the bodies of everyone in the open. Those standing next to buildings were literally nailed to the structures by the flachettes. By the time the assault force hit the ground the only surviving humans were locked in two buildings.

Hussen was trying desperately to make contact with anyone on the radio. However, for some reason unknown to him, the radio responded only with a wail of static.

The shape charges that blew the door off the communications shed, continued through the door and disemboweled Major Hussen ended his confusion and fear. The six men that rushed the room killed everyone there in less than ten seconds. Two men stayed with the equipment as the other four cleared the remaining rooms. Three minutes after entering, the building was secure.

The four teams assigned to hit the billets were done in half the time since most of the troops had been in the open when the main assault was prepped by the support team. The intelligence gathering team had finished the billets and were entering the first of the five armories as those targets were secured.

The primary target team entered from four directions at once: the main series of doors had been breached and the team leader held position for a full minute to allow a team to blow a whole in the roof and top floor rear. On a radio signal, all four teams stormed the building after dropping tear gas. Five minutes later the top two floors of the building were secure and the nuke team was setting the neutron bomb for detonation. One of the I.T. force had been wounded when a terrorist technician, who had the presence to put on a gas mask, shot him in the groin with a 9mm Chicon pistol. It was the last shot he would ever fire because he was quartered by three AK-47s.

The security team had conducted a quick sweep of the compound killing the wounded and clearing an LZ for the exfiltration.

Meanwhile, the diversionary force had left the 105s and were boogying away from the compound to give the reactionary force something to chase.

When the reactionary force from the compound heard and saw what was happening behind them there was a pause while their commander attempted to decide whether he should turn around and return to camp, or continue after the dust cloud in front of them.

He had little time to ponder before a squadron of four A-10s strafed them with 20mm cannon. When the dust settled, the entire reactionary force was nothing but a shredded banquet for the jackels and buzzards. The squadron made one final pass to take pictures of their work before overflying the diversionary force and tipping their wings.

Colonel Morse was talking to the Security Team NCO when two men from the Intelligence team came running up to him.

"Re-e-e-a-a-l good sir," responded the NCO.

"Well, wipe that shit eating grin off your face and get ready to load up. We'll debrief en route." The Colonel turned to walk away.

"Colonel, have we got room for about ten or twelve tons of extra baggage?"

"Drop the games, sport. What the fuck over?"

"Colonel, we have plenty of neat CI shit, but we also found a mini-Fort Knox."

"Say again?"

"It's hard to tell, but there's a whole fucking room full of gold."

"Christ, we'd need six CH-47's to move that much weight. We can't do it. I'm sure the Board would love the revenue, but we just can't get it out."

CSM Rucker came walking up through the dust looking like a powdered gingerbread monster. "Two of those Russki choppers will fly, Colonel. The shells are damaged, but they seem operational. Are we okay on aircraft or should I blow them now?"

Everyone except Rucker broke out into huge smiles.

"Sergeant Major, as it turns out we can use those birds. Get me the radio."

Morse quickly briefed Rucker on the plan and then picked up the radio.

"I.T. Six to Eagle over."

"This is Eagle, go Six."

"I need two chopper crews, rotary wing, on the ground over."

"Wait one, over."

"Now Eagle, over."

"You got it, Six. The first four aircraft down for come-back will deposit over."

"Tango Yankee Eagle out."

The first three aircraft landing to exfiltrate the troops each dropped off one pilot, the fourth aircraft dropped three more. Two confused three man crews were turned over to Rucker and led to the Russian helicopters. They were Russian HOOK's. Normal crew was five men per aircraft, troops capacity sixty-five to seventy men, range 620 miles.

"I don't fucking believe it," said Lieutenant Wiler.

"Believe it, son," said Rucker.

"Are we supposed to fly this beast?"

"You be a pilot, L.T., you fly helicopters. This is a helicopter. You're gonna fly it."

"What the fuck. Why not?"

The assault team had been exfiltrated leaving only the intelligence team and the security team on the ground as they helped load the two Russian HOOK helicopters with about fourteen tons of gold. As they were loading the last of it, Sergeant Ewing of the security team came running up to Colonel Morse. "Colonel, there ain't nothing left alive here except good guys and whoever locked themselves in the two basements of the NBC buildings. We announced that we were going to blow the whole magilla, but they are not responding."

"Okay, sarg, shut it down and mount up. Those poor fuckers won't ever know what hit them."

"Yes, sir!" He ran back to the building to withdraw the balance of his team.

"Sergeant Major, call in the perimeter. I'll leave on the first ship, you leave on the last."

"Yes, sir!" said Rucker as he marched back toward a smoldering building barking orders.

The two Intell sergeants who discovered the gold walked up to Morse and asked, "How much do you think we got, Colonel?"

"Well, we loaded the HOOKS to the brim with around fourteen tons of the stuff. Given the way Ingalls and the Board heavyweights deals, maybe a tad short of 180 million dollars."

"Hot damn," said the older sergeant.

"Yeah, I'm sure you two can expect a bonus off this gig. Ingalls is gonna shit a brick when he sees that stuff."

"It would have been a shame to leave it, sir."

"It should take some of his edge off over being left behind with nothing to do but watch the XO drink tea and play cribbage."

CHAPTER THIRTY-SIX

Little did Morse know that at that moment another I.T. operation was underway in a Greek airport.

The plan was classic, and simple. The assault team was comprised of two elements: attack and diversion. The diversion element was headed by a Sergeant LaChance. Ingalls had contacted the Executive Committee and arranged for LaChance to be met by an executive of the airline who would introduce LaChance and one of his men as security experts from the airline company. They would serve a dual role in that they would confuse and generally bother the local authorities while at the same time direct the assault element. Their primary function was to gain authorization for the assault element to do what was needed. What transpired during the next twenty-two minutes would be world news for months to come.

Five men from the assault element walked out onto the airstrip and engaged the terrorist leader in conversation which roughly announced that their demands were in the process of being met and that they would be informed as soon as their comrades were released and on a plane. Four men set off an explosion about 600 meters from the aircraft as a diversion, to give a helicopter an excuse to overfly the hijacked airliner. The negotiating team explained to the terrorist that there had been an accident elsewhere on the field and that the safety crews were responding to the fire with equipment in a helicopter.

Actually, the helicopter held the six man primary assault element. They rappelled from the helicopter onto the top of the airplane where they set four small charges. The small shape charges were set in series so that when detonated they all would go off at the same time. Immediately after the small explosions which resulted in four, four inch holes into the cabin, a special nerve gas which immediately incapacitated everyone on board was forced into the aircraft. From the time the men landed on the roof of the aircraft, until the entire complement of occupants, passengers, crew and terrorists were unconscious, less than two minutes had elapsed.

The assault team then rappelled down to the door which they blew open. Once inside they immediately revived one of the stewardesses with an injection of antidote, placed a gas mask on her, and had her identify the terrorists. She was escorted off the plane as the assault element proceeded to assasinate the terrorists. Each man was shot once between the eyes with a .44 caliber revolver. They stopped when they came to the man identified as the leader. Him they didn't shoot. Rather, they cut off his head with one blow of a machete. They picked up the bloody product of their handiwork, and put it in a special zippered top, heavy plastic bag. Then they exited the aircraft and were joined by Sergeant LaChance who was giving instructions to the airport officials as the assault team removed their gas masks.

''Gentlemen, everyone on the aircraft will recover within a couple of hours. You should not enter the aircraft without gas masks fitted with a special filter. I'm afraid your standard issue riot control protective masks won't work against the gas we used. It won't be safe to enter for another thirty minutes. Then it will be safe to start removing the passengers and crew."

"What about the terrorists?" asked the Greek police officer in charge of the detail.

"Oh, yes, you can remove them too," said LaChance with a grin. "They'll be waiting for you peacefully. We—uh, 'restrained' them for you."

"Mr. Wingate, we need to get going," added one of the team.

"Oh, not yet. You need to wait until we are through here. And the press is anxious to interview you." LaChance looked at his team who were showing obvious signs of wanting to get the hell out of there. Then he looked at the beaming Mr. Wingate, shrugged his shoulders and smiled his response.

"Oh, well, okay. But can we at least have a few minutes to debrief and clean up. After all if we're going to have pictures and all that we want to look good."

"Of course, gentlemen. You can use the pilots' lounge to clean up and conduct your briefings. I'll keep the press boys away until then. Say about fifteen minutes in my office?"

"That should be fine, sir," said LaChance as the teams headed for the pilots' lounge. However, before they got there, they took a detour to the cars waiting for them. They were boarding a helicopter fifteen minutes later departing Greece.

CHAPTER THIRTY-SEVEN

Morse and the entire operational detachment had landed at the Objective Rallying Point Command Post. They posted a guard around the two Soviet HOOK helicopters and were entering the debriefing room as Scott came up to them.

"Well, how did it go? We've already had reports of the explosion. Initial speculation is that Libya has just tested a nuclear device in the desert. The wires are literally abuzz."

"Mission accomplished, boss. As planned," said Morse suppressing a smile.

"Casualties?" asked Ingalls.

"One man received a 9 millimeter vasectomy and lost a lot of blood. But apparently, except for giving up his right ball, he'll be fine. In fact, he's in a bit of a hurry to field test his one remaining nut."

"Congratulations, Colonel. I'd like to see the man who was hit when it's convenient." Scott handed Morse a long Dunhill Monte Cruz Panatella.

"Sure . . . he'll be glad to see you. By the way, we had a little unexpected luck. In fact, we brought back a present that maybe you can use."

"Luck? Present? Colonel, what the hell are you talking about? Am I supposed to play twenty questions?"

"Come with me, sport." Morse led Ingalls outside to the landing zone.

"Holy shit! Those are Russian HOOK's. What the devil did you take them for?"

"Cargo."

"Colonel, would you please wipe that shit eating grin off your face and tell me in simple military terms—just what the fuck is going on? And what do you mean cargo?"

"Yes, sir, Mr. Ingalls. Oh, by the way you owe a healthy bonus to two of our Intelligence sergeants."

"If you say so, they got it. Now why the HOOK's? The Chinook wasn't good enough?"

"Scotty, those two Soviet chunks of metal each hold about seven tons of what we believe from it's composition, weight and color to be gold bullion."

"You're shitting me?"

"Not I, sir. My sphincter isn't large enough, and, were I to try to shit you, I might ruin a perfect asshole. Which by the way is just what you look like right now. Aw shit, here, look for yourself."

Scott climbed up into the nearest helicopter to view the strapped down pile of gold ingots.

"Goddamn!" He stood, mouth open staring at the pile of gold.

"No doubt he will, sport. Kind of pretty, ain't it?"

"Colonel, I'm not even going to ask right now. Shit. I send you on Mission Impossible and you come back with the Great Brinks robbery. You are really something else."

"All in a day's work. By the way we kicked more than a little ass, and the Intell team has names, dates, manifests and plans which list locations, dates—all kinds of neat shit. Now, let's pack up and get outta here. Where's the party going to be?" asked Morse as he spit out the end of the cigar and lighted it with an old beat up Zippo he dug out of his fatigue pants.

"Oh, yeah, the party. The party's all set, we have a chateau in the south of France all stocked with booze, broads and music waiting for us."

"Well, then, let's go." Morse started off for the Command Post.

"Uhmm, we have to wait about another hour or so for the others to return. Then we can leave as soon as LaChance debriefs."

"What others? Rucker was on the last bird."

"Oh, I'm sorry, Colonel. I forgot to tell you. While you were terrorizing those poor Libyan terrorists, we launched another mission to Athens."

"What?" It was Morse's turn to be look dumbfounded and surprised.

"Yeah, they are under the same radio silence you had on your return, so I haven't talked to LaChance yet, but from what we picked up from the press wires a team of unidentified men posing as Pan Am security raided a downed airliner at the Athens airport, freed over 240 passengers and crew and reportedly killed ten terrorists, decapitating one of them."

"No shit?"

"No shit." Scott took out two Dunhill Monte Cruz cigars and offered one to Morse who was beaming like a high school coach who had just won the championship.

"Scotty, I have a bottle of Dom Perignon 1957 stowed in my duffle. I've been saving it ever since we got our asses kicked out of Saigon. How about you and me icing it down and drinking it together?"

"Colonel, save that bottle until we get to France. I already have twenty-five cases of the stuff cold. It's not

'57, but it is Dom Perignon. Everyone gets his own bottle before we leave."

"You're a real classy guy, Mr. Ingalls. Balls, brains and a real classy guy."

"Yeah, I guess you're right. Come on, let's go see our wounded warrior." The two soon to be most infamous men in current events walked off toward the infirmary tent. They both shared feelings they would never articulate to each other. There was a pride and apprehension much like an NFL team after winning the Super Bowl—for now they were winners, champions. But for how long? What about tomorrow—next season? The next mission. In the game they now played, there could be no second place—no close games. No ties. They had to repeat this victory each time they acted. They had to now face a future which promised only two options: victory or death.

CHAPTER THIRTY-EIGHT

The party at the chateau was something to make both Hugh Hefner and Bob Guccione jealous. Wine, women, music, games, sun and all that good stuff. Even Cleveland Rucker was laughing and joking. While the troops partied, Scott was holding a small meeting with Colonel Morse and the Executive Committee.

"Okay, men, what's the fallout?" asked Scott.

"Well, officially, the actions are being condemned by all governments, and there are more warrants for Scott Ingalls than John Dillinger ever had. Several terrorist groups claim you and I.T. will be dead by week's end. That bit with the head was a bit too much. They are calling you 'the butcher.' However, unofficially, Washington thinks you're the slickest thing since the pre-wet rubber. Nevertheless, your old college chum Pastor is heading a Senate committee dedicated to your capture and castration."

"Well, that's kind of what we expected anyway, wasn't it?"

"The upside is there are already T-shirts, fan clubs, support from Veterans groups, the NRA and a host of people to the right of Attila the Hun. The Russians are absolutely bullshit. Although they claim they had nothing to do with the camp you hit, they refuse to comment on the samples of VX-type gas we turned over to Washington. More than a few folk are curious about where a bunch of freelancers got their hands on a neutron bomb. I hope Willy Bond didn't leave anyone exposed.''

''Conclusions?'' asked Scott.

''You certainly got the attention of a whole lot of people. People who are jealous they didn't do it, and people who want you dead last year. An awful lot of bad guys are real scared from what we can tell,'' finished Slade.

''Well, after the guys downstairs sober up, we need to move to a safe training site and gear up for the next job,'' added Morse. ''Jerry has a line on the Bill Devens incident,'' he whispered to Scott.

Scott gave Morse an approving nod.

''Scott?'' Slade seemed suddenly uncomfortable.

''Go on, Ben.''

''The Board is almost as scared as the bad guys. They want a meeting.''

''Oh?'' Scott raised an eyebrow and flipped through a file of press clippings.

''They seem to think that they should have had more input. A great many of them are concerned about the use of a nuclear device, and they keep harping on that statement you made, and the way you brandished that decapitated head.''

''Fuck 'em! What did they think we were going to do kiss the sumbitches,'' shouted Morse.

''Colonel, they feel used—and we need their financial support to continue,'' pleaded Slade.

''Ben, they were used. That's their protection. But I agree, they deserve a meet. However, a full scale board meeting would be suicide. We just can't trust that large of a meeting,'' said Scott.

"So, what are you going to do? You can't ignore them," questioned Slade.

"The hell we can't!" said Morse.

"Calm down, Colonel. Look Ben, have the committee chairmen meet at Goat Island in Newport. Once there we'll shuttle them around a bit until we get them to a secure place, and I'll meet with them. Tell them to prepare for two days." Scott was writing on a pad as he spoke.

"What are you going to tell them? You really shouldn't have shown that head the way you did," sighed Slade.

"Ben, don't worry. I'll handle it. And invite Senator Pastor too."

"Are you nuts?" chimed Morse.

"Of course, Colonel. Look, I've even got the clippings to prove it. Gentlemen, if there is nothing else right now, I promised Leslie a game of tennis and a small sexual marathon."

As Scott rose to leave, several of the Executive Committee exchanged glances. Scott left the room followed closely by Morse. As they were walking down the hall they are met by Jerry Kapstein at the top of the stairs.

"Hi, Jer! I hear you have a lead on the Devens thing. What did you turn up?" asked Scott.

"Scott, Colonel. I need a couple of minutes of your time. Something rather significant just crossed my desk." Kapstein looked like he just witnessed Treblinka.

Morse and Ingalls looked at one another and led Kapstein into a parlor overlooking the lawn.

"Shoot, Captain," said Scott.

"I've got six floppy disks of reports on the aftershock of our work. Most of it is routine, and anticipated. The fan clubs and T-shirts are kinda funny. I've heard all three networks want to talk to you about a series, and someone in Korea is doing a cartoon on our exploits. The orientals love grisly stuff. They loved the head thing."

"Get to your point, Captain," snarled Morse.

"Yes sir. Sorry about that. Well, it seems that in the wake of our muscle flexing, and your video debut, a rather unholy alliance has surfaced."

Both Scott and Morse furrowed their brows and stared at Kapstein.

"Reportedly, the CIA, KGB, British Intelligence, and my old alma mater the Mossad, have agreed to a joint venture to pick you up."

"What?" Morse was more visibly upset than Scott had ever seen him.

"You mean they'll cooperate in hitting me?"

"No sir. Not a hit. They want you alive, but they want you—and bad." Kapstein looked into Scott's eyes and swore he could see a glint—like the sun reflecting off a diamond.

"How?" asked Scott in a very calm voice.

"That's unclear, sir, but allegedly, they have someone on the Executive Committee who has agreed to help." On saying this, Kapstein could not maintain eye contact, so he looked at his feet.

"I don't believe it. The Board sure, but not the Executive Committee." Now it was Scott's turn to look upset.

"This info is 24 karat, gentlemen. Plus all indications are, this is the group that planted Bill Devens."

"Well, that sure as shit explains a lot," growled Morse.

"I suggest you do a David Copperfield and disappear for a while," said Kapstein.

"No, I don't think so, Jer. You keep on it. Assemble the staff after dinner tonight and I'll tell you how we are going to handle this.'' Scott turned and started to walk away from his two friends.

''With kid gloves and a very big hammer would be good way, sir,'' said Kapstein at the departing figure of Scott.

''That's kind of what I had in mind, Jer. Colonel, come with me please. Jer, would you tell Leslie, I need a rain check on the tennis game. I'll see her for cocktails at five.''

''You got it, boss.''

CHAPTER THIRTY-NINE

Calvin Pastor walked through his front door and dropped his brief case and coat on the chair in the front hall. As he walked into the study, his wife came out of the kitchen.

"You're home early. Is something wrong?" She kissed him gently on the cheek.

"Oh, no. Absolutely everything is fine—wonderful. Then again everything is totally, totally fucked at the same time." He poured himself a brandy from a bottle of Armagnac.

"Oh, I see. Everything is fine, and wrong, and you are having a drink at three in the afternoon."

"I met with the President this morning," he said looking into his brandy snifter, not at his wife.

"My, that's exciting. Does he want to endorse you for his job?" she smiled.

"You know what he said?"

"I'm sure you're about to tell me."

"He said: 'Go through the options with your committee, Cal, but don't lean on this Ingalls thing too hard.' Can you fucking believe it? He thinks Scott is some grand solution to the problem no one else can handle." He gulped down the brandy and slammed the glass on a coffee table.

"Oh." Jennifer's response was almost a whisper.

"Oh, indeed. I attempted to suggest that Scotty, my old friend and college buddy, was an international criminal on the same par with the terrorists he claims he wants to rid the world of. But the President said 'strictly off the record, Senator, extreme evil requires extreme actions.' Can you fucking believe it. The President of the United States was actually condoning Scott and his band of merry murders, and paraphrasing Scott to me."

There was an awkward pause in which the only noise which disturbed the silence was the gentle music of Zamfir's pan flute playing on a CD unit in the kitchen.

"Steven wants an I.T. T-shirt," Jennifer said.

"What?"

"You heard me. Your son wants an I.T. T-shirt—the one with Uncle Scott's picture on it."

"Absolutely not! I will not have my son promoting a criminal. What the hell is going on? Am I being punished for bad karma I collected in some awful past life? Is Rod Serling standing on the stairs? Am I the only sane fucking person left in this screwy world? Or is Scott being confused for the patron saint of vigilantes?"

"Cal, calm down. At the risk of getting my head bitten off, might I suggest that you are taking this entire I.T. thing entirely too personally?"

"You're damn right I'm taking it personally. Scott tried to get me involved, then he got me drunk and drew information from me to help him. Jennifer, he cannot be allowed to take the law into his own hands. And I can't support him no matter how twisted his motives might be." Cal poured himself another drink.

"Cal, maybe this time the law was better off in his hands than with the more conventional authorities."

"Now you? First the President, then my son and now my own wife turns against me?"

"Cal . . ."

"Don't Cal me. Those hands in which you would entrust the law did a nice job with the head of that terrorist didn't he? You want our son looking up to a man like that—let alone have to see that kind of stuff? I'd rather have him sit through a weekend of Charles Bronson and Clint Eastwood than thirty seconds with 'his uncle Scott.' "

"What are you going to do, Senator?"

Cal collected himself and sipped form his glass. Then he gently placed the glass on the bar, and after a brief moment in which he took a very deep breath he turned to face his wife.

"You know what I'm going to do? I'm going to do the only reasonable and right thing to do. Exactly what the President told me to do. Go through the motions but not lean on Ingalls. It's the only politically expedient thing to do. Shit, the son of a bitch could probably run for office and beat me, or the President if he chose. He's gathering quite a constituency. Maybe I should get an I.T. T-shirt myself." He half smiled.

"Tell you what, Senator Pastor—you're three hours late, but how about a three o'clock nooner?" Jennifer smiled and walked up to put a hand on her husband's shoulder.

He smiled at his wife and put the cork in the brandy. "Sure thing, lady. Then I can do to you what everybody else has been doing to me all day."

CHAPTER FORTY

Jerry Kapstein dialed the number Scott had given him for Senator Pastor's private line in his home study. It was about ten in the evening Eastern Standard time when he called. The phone rang four times before it was picked up.

"Hell-o?" Calvin answered the phone himself.

"Senator Calvin Pastor?"

"Yes, who's calling?"

"Senator, I am calling for Mr. Scott Ingalls. He would like to invite you to a meeting."

"What?"

"I said, Mr. Ingalls would like to invite you to a meeting."

"Why? So he can cut off my head like that terrorist fellow?"

"Senator, I assure you, Mr. Ingalls has personally guaranteed your safety. He says to tell you he realizes you are merely doing a job, as is he. He merely desires to afford you the opportunity to hear from him personally his side of a very complex story."

"I used to know Scott Ingalls. He was a very bright, sensitive and talented man. I ceased knowing him when we parted company at Harvard and he joined the Army. I have known another Scott Ingalls since I came to office, but I certainly do not know the Scott Ingalls who cuts off heads and sets off nuclear bombs."

Scott reached across the desk to take the phone from Kapstein.

"Cal, don't be a horse's ass," said Scott.

"Scott?"

"Listen, Senator, you are heading the Senate committee investigating my activities. I am prepared to provide you with first hand testimony—right from the horse's mouth."

"My, we are just full of equine metaphor today aren't we?" said Calvin.

"Cal . . ."

"Scott, do you have any idea of the impact of what you have done?"

"I believe so, Senator."

"Don't Senator me, Scott. My own sons wants a fucking I.T. T-shirt. My wife thinks you can do a better job of what you do than the governments of the world. Jesus Christ, Scott, the fucking President of the United States implied to me off the record he thinks you're the slickest thing since Kris Kringle."

There was a long pause.

"Scott, what you are doing is wrong. Had we talked more, and examined your plans, maybe we could have worked out something for you with the CIA or the Delta Force people—but you have already gone too far. You are in some heavy shit, my friend—and way out of your league."

"Cal, do you, as Chairman of the Senate investigating committee, want to talk to me?"

"No . . . I don't want to talk to you—or see you—or even acknowledge I ever knew you. But, as Chairman of the committee, I suppose I have a responsibility to do just that. I don't suppose you'd want to come into my office or appear before the committee?"

"Cal . . ."

"Okay. I didn't think so. But I'm not going to meet you in some dark warehouse or deserted dock."

"Day after tomorrow. Take a plane to Logan. Grab a cab to South Station. Take the T to North Station and get on the North Shore train. Get off in Beverly. You'll be met by a driver who will take you to Salem."

"That North Shore train is a crime."

"Talk to your Representative. I'll see you in a couple of days. Cal, be there—and don't bring anyone—in fact don't tell anyone, not even Jennifer. If you are followed, I won't be there, pal."

"It's just like you, Scott, to bring a witch hunt to Salem."

"Bye!"

Colonel Morse sat next to Kapstein opposite Ingalls' desk.

"Sport, this may well be the dumbest thing a smart man ever did."

CHAPTER FORTY-ONE

The meeting of the unholy alliance was taking place in an old farmhouse outside of Williamsburg, Virginia. Present for the meeting was a strange collection of fierce rivals: Brent Garfield, CIA; David Rosenburg, Mossad; Ivan Gorky, KGB; and, Harrison Wolf, MI5.

"Gentlemen, I am as surprised by this meeting as any of you. However, we are all in the same business, and we all take orders from men with a larger overview than any of us. We have been instructed to cooperate in this Ingalls matter, and to develop a plan for capturing him. We have been ordered to make every effort to take him alive, but should that prove impossible, we must eliminate his leadership role in this I.T. thing." Brent Garfield was chairing the meeting by merit of home court advantage.

"I, for one, am anxious to cooperate in the true spirit of *glasnost*," said Gorky.

"Bullshit!" said Rosenburg. "Let's keep to the key elements: first none of us trusts the other—fact; second, our team play in this gig is designed to protect our organizations and not closet anyone from taking credit for crushing this I.T.; and, third, if any of us get a chance to fuck the others professionally, we will. Is that clearly stated enough and more or less accurate?"

"Jews used to be such great diplomats. All that American blood has tainted your race. You are so direct—and offensive." Wolf was speaking while filling his pipe with a heavy English blend which included about one third Latikea, which would overpower the room in minutes.

"Hey, guys, lighten up will you?" Garfield was trying to restore order.

"We all know we don't like each other, or trust each other, and are all a bit surprised our bosses have us in the same room armed and don't want us to kill one another. If we all share intelligence, just on this Ingalls thing, and perform our tasks as assigned, we should be able to knock off this job in a week, and get back to screwing over each other."

"Very well, Mr. Garfield, where do we begin?" asked Wolf.

"We should have two real clean shots at him within the next week. The tap we have on Senator Pastor's home phone picked up a conversation yesterday which had Ingalls inviting Pastor to a meet," said Garfield.

"You mean you tapped a U.S. Senator's telephone?" asked Gorky.

"Every day, pal. You didn't think the Russkies had a corner on that market did you? We'll use three, three person phase lines to cover the Senator. One group will cover from his home to the airport, another picks him up at Logan to South Station. Another from South Station through the Boston T to North Station. Three people ride the train with him to Beverly and continue to the end of the line. Another team will pick up in Beverly and follow to wherever the final meet is. We have stationed a boat in Marblehead and one off Ipswich. I have a compound secured on the Cape at Camp Edwards. It's a National Guard facility on Otis Air Force Base. It's so desolate that thieves once ripped off all the copper plumbing one winter and no one noticed for three months.''

''What if we are spotted?'' asked Rosenburg.

''This is a gimmee. We didn't expect this to happen. If we score, so much the better, we can all go back to our jobs sooner. If it busts, we still have our trump card. We have a man on the I.T. Executive Committee and he tells us there will be a meeting of that group with Ingalls and Colonel Morse next week. We have arranged so that we can track our man, and then hit the meeting site with a rapid deployment team.''

''Why not just wait for that meeting?'' asked Wolf.

''Hey pal, I might be chairing this meeting, but I don't give the orders. I take them, just like you. Apparently, somebody thinks security will be lighter on the Pastor meet than the Executive Committee get together.''

''I doubt it,'' said Gorky.

''Me too,'' said Rosenburg.

''Based on the two operations this group has already conducted, I rather doubt they will tend to be sloppy. After all our planning and work, they still discovered our Bill Devens switch. Reportedly, he threw together that Athens raid in less than an hour. These blokes are good,'' noted Wolf.

''Well, we just have to be better. The plan and assignments are in those binders. Please open them and let's go over task assignments,'' grunted Garfield.

CHAPTER FORTY-TWO

Kapstein, Morse and Ingalls sat in a study in the French chateau with cigars, brandy and headaches.

"Scott, we have three recommendations for you to take under advisement—as long as you agree to agree," said Kapstein with his ever present smile.

"Jerry . . ."

"Goddamn it, Ingalls, stop relying on your luck and charm. If you insist on going to those wells too often, you're gonna end up dead,' said Morse.

"Hey, guys, I promise to listen. I don't promise to agree. Go ahead."

"Okay," Morse signaled. "Go ahead, Captain."

"Well, there are basically three elements to our input to you, boss. First, don't go ahead with the plastic surgery. Consensus is that you can achieve just as much with disguises and the like as with a face change. You can't change certain basics like your finger prints, blood type, voice print, etc. There is a certain element of advantage in maintaining you as the visible spokesperson for I.T. We need a consistent focus and identity in order to maintain continuity, and all our research and analysis is that you are already established as The Man so we might as well exploit that. Bottom line is: No identity-altering surgery for Ingalls.''

''Okay, I'll buy off on that. As long as you and the Colonel recognize that you will have the additional job responsibility of keeping me warm and breathing.''

''What do you mean 'additional?' It's an implied task right now, thank you very much.''

''Second, cancel the Pastor meeting. We have learned that his phone is tapped which means, the bad guys probably already know about your meeting on the North Shore. For you to meet with him would virtually guarantee compromising security and probably getting you nailed,'' Kapstein continued.

''Acknowledged, and noted. However, I'm still going to meet with Cal. If we know there is likely to be company, you'll just have to plan for it and compensate. Cal may be a pompous horse's ass, but he deserves this one time only face-to-face with me.''

''Goddamn it, Scott,'' groaned Morse.

''There's no goddamn it about it—I meet with the Senator. You guys just work harder to keep me alive.''

''You don't make it easy, pal,'' added Morse.

''I never promised you a rose garden Colonel. That's two. You're batting 500—what's number three.''

''Cancel the Executive Committee meeting,'' Kapstein said and locked his eyes on those of his boss.

''No way, Clyde,'' said Scott.

''We've got the rotten apple narrowed down to two, but we can't confirm who the snitch is, or why. If you won't cancel—at least postpone until we can verify who the bogy is—please,'' pleaded Kapstein.

''Can we talk?'' asked Scott.

''Ingalls, Joan Rivers you ain't. We simply will not

allow you to walk into an Executive Committee ambush until we know who ratted. If need be, I think I can still kick your ass and hog tie you," argued Morse.

"Tell you what. Bump the meeting one week. Arrange for the members to be flown to the site in Cozumel. Require them all to arrive at the launch in bathing suits and sandals. No chance of wires or concealed anything. Between us we should be able to narrow down two suspects to the one guilty party," smiled Scott.

"And if we can't?" asked Kapstein.

"Then I handle it in the meeting."

"I don't like it, sport,'" responded Morse.

"I don't like it, either. But that's the way it goes. You have one week to ID which of your two suspects is the leak. Regardless of your results, I meet with the Committee at the end of that week. I'm betting this gaggle of heroes can solve the problem before I have to."

"Deal," said Morse looking at Kapstein who was shaking his head and looking concerned.

CHAPTER FORTY-THREE

"Our Executive Committee informant will be fitted with a small transmitter in a right rear molar. It will be mostly plastic, with so little metal as to pass for a filling should he be scanned," noted Garfield to the men around the table.

"What happens when we bust in?" asked Wolf.

"Everyone except Ingalls dies."

"Including our informant?" asked Gorky.

"Especially our informant," sighed Garfield.

CHAPTER FORTY-FOUR

Senator Pastor grabbed his cashmere overcoat with the Burberry lining and kissed his wife good-bye.

"I have a meeting in Boston this afternoon. I should be back tomorrow for supper, hon."

"Who are you meeting?" she asked as she helped him on with his overcoat.

"I can't say," he said buttoning up the coat front.

"Calvin, if I didn't know you better, I'd think you had a woman on the side."

"Jen, you know I'd never do anything like that. Besides, I don't like it on the side: top, bottom, front, back, sure—but never on the side."

"It's about Scott, isn't it?" she asked.

There was a short pregnant pause during which they both stared at each other. Then he broke the mood of tension by smiling and saying, "How about a pork roast with acorn squash for dinner?"

"Sure, Senator," and she rushed up and hugged him hard.

"You just be careful . . ."

"Jennifer, the boy wonder Senator is always careful. See you on the morrow." He closed the front door and moved toward the waiting limo.

Calvin flew to Logan airport and ended up sitting next to one of the senior vice presidents from John Hancock Insurance who ragged on him during the entire flight about the proposed tax reform bill currently being debated on the Senate floor. It was a pain in the ass, but it served well to take his mind off the I.T. affair. At Logan he took a cab to South Station and immediately walked down to the T where he bought a token and entered the labyrinth of big city mass transportation system. As he boarded the first car it struck him that although he had not ridden the T since college, they had not changed appreciably. When he arrived at North Station he walked up into the cold through conversations of Celtics superiority. He purchased his ticket to Beverly and walked out to the train which was departing in just ten minutes.

He was likewise amazed to find that the trains had not changed since college. They were still dreary and dirty. The windows were dulled with smoke stains and grime. He tried to doze off, realizing that this train would stop at every podunk town from Boston to Lynn to Peabody to Beverly/Danvers.

About the only saving grace to this ride was it eventually ended in Salem and Marblehead, both of which were lovely, especially in the pre and post tourist spring and autumn. His musings were interrupted when the conductor walked down the aisle chanting "Next stop Beverly." He collected his coat and briefcase and got off the train. As he panned the station he spotted a large black Lincoln limousine with a tall bulky black man holding open a door. He walked to the limo.

"Senator, right this way please," said the driver with what appeared to be a slight Jamaican accent.

Once seated, the driver told him that there was coffee

and brandy in the bar. He poured himself a brandy, noting it was a new bottle of Remy Martin. The phone rang, and he picked it up.

"Hello, Senator. Nice trip?" asked Scott.

"No, it wasn't a nice trip. It sucked. As I suspected, neither the T nor the trains have changed—they are both criminal. And yes, I intend to talk to my Representative."

Pause.

"Well, what now, Scotty? Am I to meet a Moroccan with a fez and red carnation in his lapel?"

"Nothing that Bogart, Cal. However, there is a slight snag."

"Snag? What do you mean? I didn't suffer through this for a snag."

"You are being followed, Senator. And quite professionally, I might add."

"Impossible! No one knows we are meeting."

"Were that that were true. However, the fact is that you have been followed since we picked you up at Logan. Three man teams that change at each dogleg. Someone knew exactly the instructions I gave you."

"Impossible!"

"They probably had your phone tapped."

"They? Who are they? No one would dare tap my phone."

"Cal, don't be naive. Of course they would dare. And they have. Just sit tight. We are about to teach your escorts not to meddle in our business and not to fuck with the phone of a U.S. Senator." The phone went dead.

"Hold on Senator," said the driver.

POW! FLAP, FLAP, FLAP, SCREECH. . . .

The driver had pushed a small button on a tan box on the front seat, blowing the right rear tire. When this happened the car in front and two cars behind also stopped. What happened next happened very quickly. Three four man teams in vans pulled up to the three cars and jumped out. With shotguns they shot out the tires of the lead and trail vehicles which were tagging them. Two of the drivers attempted to get out and return fire but were shot with laser guns immediately, non-lethally putting them down. The third driver remained in his car, dropped his gun out the window and waved, placing both hands on the window. A blue Mercedes 300 Turbo pulled up next to the limo and the rear door opened.

"Climb aboard, Senator." They rushed Calvin into the back seat and sped off. The car drove through Salem into Marblehead and out onto a long causeway. Once there Calvin was escorted to an open boat and driven to an airplane sitting on the water. He climbed aboard to find Scott, Colonel Morse, and Jerry Kapstein.

"Welcome home, Cal," said Ingalls with a smile as he started the plane to take off.

Kapstein took the attache case and proceeded to examine it and its contents. Morse proceeded to pat down the Senator by grabbing handfulls of clothing and crushing them in his hand.

"Nothing here, sir," said Kapstein

"He's clean, sport," echoed Morse. "Sorry about the creases, Senator."

"Scott, what is the meaning of all this?"

"Senator, right now a consortium of the CIA, KGB, Mossad and MI5 is trying to get their hands on me. They apparently tried to use you to do that. We just stopped them."

"Preposterous!" responded Pastor without a great deal of conviction.

"Cal, I wanted to meet with you, against all the advice of my colleagues for a variety of reasons. Eventually, someone will kill me. However, I intend to postpone that eventuality as long as possible."

"Scott . . ."

"No. You listen—I talk. You said what I am doing is wrong. Perhaps so. However, for whatever convoluted reasons I harbor, it is important to me that you hear me out. You never understood why I left Harvard to fight in a war no one wanted. You thought I should have stayed, gone into business, developed and, like you, prospered. I thought that was what I wanted too. Then my folks died, and my grandmother died of an empty heart shortly thereafter. I had no family to speak of, and was forced to reassess my life and what I could do with it. I probably went into the Army for all the wrong reasons. I was running away—I was angry, frightened, and empty. Maybe I had a death wish. However, as Colonel Morse will tell you, besides mastering certain taught skills, I am cursed with being uncommonly lucky. I should have died a dozen times in Nam. But I didn't. When I came back and hit New York, I should have had my butt kicked dozens of times in deals—but it wasn't. Along the way I became the product of my experiences. And my experiences were eclectic: A-team commander; ad agency account supervisor; marketing consultant; wheeler-dealer. Cal, right now, for the first time in my life, I am doing what I should be doing. I can make a difference, Cal. I may do what appears to be bad things, but they are done for the good of the order. I don't give a shit one way or another if terrorists face off in some desert and cut the shit out of one another. That kind of activity only helps reduce the population of scum. But when terrorists ply their trade, they do it among innocent people. They realize, even if governments refuse to, that as long as they employ the guerrilla tactics of hit, run and hide, there is very little conventional forces can do. They hide behind and use the very principles of ethics and morality which they assault. They are allowed to do that because governments are bogged down in diplomacy, committees, and rhetoric. Most terrorist activity, if directed against a particular country does not take place in that country. That means that the assaulted government must seek the approval and authority of the host country to take any action. This is seldom ever in coming. Host countries tend to become annoyed when the big bad rich United States attempts to do something military on their soil. Part of the problem is national hubris, part of it is petty crap. I offer a solution, and hopefully a deterrent. They can kill each other off as much as they want. But if one stray bullet hits a civilian's home, or one disinterested party is inconvenienced, we will be there to kick ass and take names. And we'll be there quick."

"Scott, you did this all wrong."

"Oh?"

"You should have talked to me, or the CIA, or your old friends in the Army. You could have been a saving grace instead of an out of control renegade."

"Cal, come on. Do you really think we ever could have gotten I.T. out of committee? We put the Athens strike together in an hour. A committee would have taken a month. No—this is the only way."

"You know they'll get you."

"They, Cal?"

"Some, they. Scott, besides pissing off the bad guys, you are making every agency and government who can't do what you do look bad. They can't allow you to continue."

"Fuck 'em!" grunted Morse. "Lead, follow, or get the fuck out of the way."

Calvin ignored Morse's outburst and turned back to Scott.

"Scott, turn yourself in, and offer to coordinate this I.T. thing with the world powers. Christ, everyone practically already agrees with what you did. But no one can afford to openly condone this 'vigilante' activity which is so blatantly criminal."

"I don't think so, Cal. Besides, I'm too cute for jail and I already have hemorrhoids."

"Scott, what are you going to do?"

"Cal, I'm going to do what I do well. I will continue to plan, coordinate and manage the world-wide activities of International Terrorist Suppressors. We will seek out terrorists and terrorize them. It may not be a good solution, by your standards, but its the only game in town right now that seems to work."

"Scott, I may not be able to stop you or influence you, but perhaps you can answer one question for real."

"If I can, Cal."

"I've heard all your rhetoric, and can see your commitment, but I still don't know the real why. What made you do it? Why have you thrown away everything for this crusade? What was the spark?"

"Senator, that's three questions."

"Scott . . ."

"Tell you what, pal, the people who provided your escort today are going to get one more shot at me next week. If I walk away from that—and I intend to walk away from that—I'll tell you then what even Colonel Morse doesn't know."

Morse looked at Kapstein who shrugged his shoulders.

"Now, in about ten minutes we will fly over Nantucket. Does your aunt still have that place on the beach? Well, I'm getting out, at about a thousand feet. Jerry Kapstein here will fly you to Block Island where you will be met by a car at the airport and driven to Old Harbor and put on the ferry to Point Judith. Another car will meet you there and take you to Providence in time for the shuttle to D.C. Give my best to Jennifer and Steven." Scott moved to the back of the plane and put on a parachute.

Pastor turned to Kapstein and asked him as Morse joined Scott in the exercise of putting on a parachute, "Do you guys get off on this international hide and seek stuff or what?"

"Senator, it sure beats punching a clock." He pushed the plane into a gradual dive leveling off at 1,000 feet.

"Cal, it was good seeing you. We may not have accomplished anything today, but I enjoyed, as always, the chance to talk with you. We may not be able to see each other for some time, but I will talk to you from time to time. Take care, pal."

Scott opened the rear door and jumped out into the wind to be followed shortly by Morse.

CHAPTER FORTY-FIVE

Scott drifted into a large field and pulled down on his toggles to execute a perfect stand up landing. He was out of his chute and S-folding it into an aviator's kit bag when Morse duplicated his landing some twenty feet upwind. Morse pulled off his chute, dropped it on the ground and walked up to Scott.

"Just what the fuck did that accomplish, sport?" he asked matter of factly.

"Colonel, how long do you think we can continue to operate?"

"The good Lord willing and the creek don't rise—indefinitely—five or ten years like falling off a log. The longer we succeed, the easier it will get."

"How much heat do you think we'll have in, say, six or seven years?"

"A lot. More at first—then less. Why?"

"Colonel, I believe that within the next six years Calvin Pastor will run for and win the Presidency of the United States."

"Come on . . ."

"No, I'm serious. He is young, good looking, more or less a middle of the roader, very bright, has an outstanding support team, and as the son of the former speaker, he is far more connected than many with three times his time in grade."

"And that's why you stroke him?"

"That's part of it. If he gets in the White House, I think we can work with him. Think of what we do and will do. How much more efficient and easy would it be if we could marshall unlimited air support? Naval support, full access to U.S. Intelligence information without having to wheel, deal, and scam to get day old satellite and Blackbird photos? Wouldn't you like to do a map recon of an objective with information that is current? Remember Son Tay? The only thing that fucked up that deal was outdated intelligence. Cal is our long term trump card, Colonel. It may not seem that way now, but he is potentially our greatest ally."

"He'll never win, and if he does, he sure as shit won't help," said Morse.

"Oh, he'll win. He has everything and more than JFK had. Money, looks, a powerful family, political connections—plus he doesn't fuck around. He's inimitably loyal to his wife and family; he's not Catholic but a nice safe vanilla Congregationalist; he was the youngest United Way Chairman in the history of the Commonwealth; he's big with Boy Scouts; and, a rabid Social Security supporter. The guy will win—and when the time is right—he'll help."

"Whatever. In the meantime, until he does win—if he does win—I need to keep you alive so we can continue to do our number. Here comes LaChance. Let's get out of here and see if we can't find out who your Executive Committee rat is." The two men walked from the field to the waiting Jeep on the dirt road.

CHAPTER FORTY-SIX

Leslie was lying on her right side cradled in Scott's arms. Scott was on his back and his left hand toyed with her hair as she ran one fingernail through the hair on his chest.

"Ya know, Scott, when this all started back in Newport, I figured it was just another one of your grandiose ideas that would never get out of your computer or away from the dinner table."

"Surprise!"

"Yeah—it sure is that."

"You having regrets on me now?" asked Scott.

"To tell you the truth I haven't been this jazzed ever! But I have to confess—I am a little scared."

Scott turned over on his left side and eased Leslie onto her back. "Babe, you'd be totally insane if you weren't more than a little scared. There will be times when your life will be in very real jeopardy."

"Hey, you're talking to a woman who jaywalks in New York."

"Seriously. We are going to have to be very careful about our time together. As long as we are at a secure R & R site like this, you'll be safe. But from now on we can't travel together, and you will have to publicly disavow and disassociate yourself from me."

"Faithless bitch! You trying to get rid of me, Ingalls?"

"No way, babe—just the opposite. I'm trying to be sure that you stay around. But a few basic elements have dramatically changed."

"Yeah. I can see a gray hair on your chest."

"Les, I am more than just a fugitive. There are some very bad people looking to do me some real heavy duty harm."

"You are invincible." She threw both arms around him.

"Wish that was true. Hon, you are going to have to come to grips with the fact that I will probably eventually be killed."

"I don't want to think about that."

"Oh, but you need to think about that. You see babe I have been very selfish with you."

"I thought that was my specialty."

"Come on, Les. You can play the hardboiled bitch with the others. This is Scott, remember?"

"You're leading somewhere," she said as she reached for a cigarette.

"Babe, I love you. I don't think I ever said that before—but I truly love you. The problem is I can't offer you all those things a man is supposed to offer a woman in return for love."

"Scott, I never really thought I would hear you say that. Of course, you know I love you. I have over ten years. I just never thought I'd hear those words from you. Now that I have, I am really scared. I don't know whether this is a beginning or an ending—and I don't want that ending right now."

"Leslie, the ending will be when someone succeeds in

blowing me away. I just want you to understand that although I love you more deeply than I have ever loved anyone, we can never marry, and we're going to be forced to be more discreet, circumspect and conniving than a Presidential candidate having an interracial homosexual affair with a retarded minor."

"Just promise me that until someone shoots your balls off, you'll continue to make love to me."

"That my love is the one commitment to you I can make."

"Then stop talking and prove it."

After they finished a frenzied session of love making, Leslie got up and went to the bathroom where she sat on the john and quietly cried for ten minutes. She would have been astounded to know that her tears were matched with those of Scott who was on his back staring up at the ceiling.

CHAPTER FORTY-SEVEN

The I.T. staff was meeting in Northern California in preparation for the upcoming Executive Committee meeting. They were in a small duck club about ten miles north of Gridley and ten miles west of the Oroville afterbay. The clubhouse they were in was a six bedroom cabin resting up on stilts. The living room consisted of a wet bar, a wood burning stove, a color television, two couches and a half dozen easy chairs. The clubhouse backed up onto Howard Slough and was hidden from aerial observation by a canopy of trees.

Bullerwell was conducting the meeting and passed out information packets. "We have completed most of our work on the Executive Committee. Three of them would most certainly die before they compromised anything we are doing. Ben Slade has a very old and faded tattoo on his right calf that says 'Death Before Dishonor,' apparently an old 101st Airborne souvenir. All indications are he really means it. Chase is even more fervent than Slade. He'd give up his mother before Scott. Danforth is just a *skoshe* behind Slade in loyalty and commitment. However, he was the only man, who when the balloon went up on

Scott, informed his Board that he had made the decision to fund I.T., and if they didn't like it they could fire him and compete against him. The entire brokerage house rolled over for him.

Lasser and Moore are the two possibles. They are the two youngest, and possibly the two most ambitious. They each made it in different ways. Moore was both brilliant and lucky. His timing on the computer boom was perfect. A year earlier no one would listen to him, and a year later he would have been eaten by IBM, ITT or some other initialed monster. Lasser could have taught Machiavelli how to write the book. He's one of those guys no one likes, but everyone invites to parties. He bought his first radio station in a leveraged buyout of the man who gave him a ten percent equity position instead of money. Two years later he buried his old benefactor. He started a weekly shopper-type rag in the midwest and within eighteen months had cornered all the food store lineage from the daily newspapers and delivered 100% of the marketplace homes, practically unheard of in the advertising game. Eventually, he bought out the two daily newspapers and turned his shopper into an insert. According to the Big Eight accounting firm's research departments he also enjoys the greatest profit margins in the industry. This kid was breaking unions before Reagan ever thought of challenging the Air Traffic Controllers."

"Talk to me about motive and opportunity," asked Scott.

"They both have had opportunity," responded Kapstein. "They each have traveled to the Orient and Europe since we started. Moore just cut a deal with the republic of China for computer technology in which he traded hardware and consulting for coal and silk. Lasser has been in Japan with the Sony R & D people on and off for the past year and a half."

"Okay so they both had opportunity to be compromised. Shit, that could happen in CONUS. What we really need to know are the whys," Morse said.

"Why not just subject the committee to the same tests we've all taken? Polygraph and chemicals will tell us all we need to know," said Xing.

"That's an alternative and no doubt the easiest way, but I want to ambush the fucker and deliver a message to that unholy alliance," said Scott.

"With all due respect, Mr. Ingalls," Ouelette said, "do you not always tell us to look at strengths and weaknesses and to reduce threats to the least common denominator?"

"Hear, hear, Jean Paul," chanted Morse.

"Gentlemen, if I may?" Kapstein spoke up.

"Yes, Jer?" asked Scott.

"I believe I have an alternative that offers the best of both worlds. We can isolate and interrogate each of the two suspects so as not to permit them knowledge they have been interrogated, and have the meeting/ambush with complete certitude of who the bad apple is."

"You have our attention, Jer—talk!" nodded Scott.

And the G-2 of I.T. proceeded to outline his plan for identifying the mole in the Executive Committee to the I.T. staff.

"You devious Jew-bastard son of a bitch," shouted Morse. "I love it!"

"Yeah, it is good, Jer. Can Xing get those people?"

"As we speak it shall be done, sir," said Xing.

"Okay. We proceed as outlined. Willy, what's for lunch?"

"Pheasant, brown rice and asparagus with hollandaise."

"You didn't shoot those pheasant out of season, did you?" chided Ingalls.

"Hey, if we're going to flip off the CIA, KGB, the Mossad and the British Secret Service I figure we can afford to challenge California Fish and Game too."

CHAPTER FORTY-EIGHT

Kapstein's plan called for LTC Xing to provide two Ninjas to accompany two of Kapstein's men. Lasser was taken in his sleep aboard a yacht in the Isthmus on the east side of Catalina Island, off Los Angeles. He was drugged, interrogated, conditioned, and left. When he woke up at six the next morning still lying in his bed, in the master cabin, with his female companion of the night before, neither he nor his paramour had any knowledge of what happened, and only mild curiosity about their respective pin pricks which itched slightly.

Moore was taken in a sensory deprivation tank. One of those Lilly tanks which came into, and left, vogue in the early seventies. He also had no knowledge of what had happened or what he had spilled. He had a slight ache in his arm where he had received a B-12 shot the day before.

When the reports were delivered to Kapstein he smiled and placed them in a plain manila envelope which he hand carried to Scott.

"Son of a bitch!" said Scott as he read the reports.

"Yeah, I lost a hundred dollar bet with Sid, but it had an upside," cried Kapstein.

"And what was that?"

"The shit talked about arranging the Bill Devens mole with the alliance. At least I now know how and why. I gotta tell you, boss, that was driving me nuts."

"Okay, let's get ready for the meeting. It's time someone learned that 'payback is a bitch.' "

CHAPTER FORTY-NINE

Garfield was presiding over the meeting. No one had talked about the failed attempt to trail Senator Pastor for the meet with Ingalls in Salem. However, they were all upset, and impressed with the obvious intelligence and tactical abilities of I.T. Additionally, they each suspected the other as having compromised the first operation in some way.

"In the interest of improving our security gentlemen, we have been authorized to keep the details of this operation within this room, and this room only. We will not report to our superiors or subordinates. We will issue orders to the men needed for only that portion of the operation which directly involves them. They will get detailed tasking assignments, but not know how they figure into the overall plan. If this operation fails because of a security leak, I will be the only possible source, and will no doubt be dead before any of you have a chance to lodge a complaint."

"I like that part," said Gorky.

"I rather thought you would, you communist son of a bitch," snarled Garfield.

"Now, now Brent, let's not get testy," chided Wolf.

"Okay. The recon elements will pick up the target at the Line of Departure. We will track our man electrically from the LD to the meeting place. The assault team will consist of twenty men armed with 9mm Uzi's and equipped with gas masks. We are going to mimic their Athens gambit with nerve gas and speed. Each of you will task five operatives to take part in the assault. Remember. Everyone except Ingalls must die. We will fly the strike force along the same doglegs our target takes. Fifteen minutes after they stop moving, we will converge on the site and do the job. Here are the details." Brent Garfield proceeded to outline what was no doubt the most important mission he had ever bet his life.

Meanwhile, less than six hundred miles away, I.T. was at work. The initial contract team consisted of six I.T. Operational Force people sent to meet the committee. They started in Atlanta and flew out to the Carolinas, stopping briefly on one of the small out-islands off Virginia Beach. Next, they flew to a small landing strip in Delonica, Georgia; then on to Louisiana. In Louisiana, they changed aircraft and flew to Jacksonville, Florida. There they were joined by Kapstein, Morse and Ingalls for a brief meeting.

"Gentlemen, I apologize for the inconvenience, but since my meeting with Senator Pastor it has become obvious we are being tracked by some heavy muscle. Therefore, I regret that for the remainder of your trip you will all have to be sedated," said Scott.

"Now see here, Scott," complained Moore, "isn't this all going a bit too far?"

"Not at all, Byron. It's necessary, or else we wouldn't do it," said Scott.

"Well, I for one could use the rest. Shoot me up," said Slade.

Sergeant LaChance stepped forward and administered an

injection to each of the Board members. Five minutes later they were on a plane and moving. Following in a DC 10, Brent Garfield and the strike force watched watches.

"False alarm. They are moving again," said Garfield. "They're going west again."

Three hours later, the Executive Committee started to wake up in a large room with four walls of glass overlooking the ocean. An NCO poured coffee for the Executives as they came around.

"Welcome to Cozumel, gentlemen. We are on a small island between the Yucatan peninsula of Mexico and the Cuba. Arguably the best bill fishing in the world."

"What the fuck?" complained Ross Lasser.

"You may suffer slight discomfort for a little while, Mr. Lasser. It was necessary for us to remove that molar of yours with the transmitter. That tooth is right now probably landing in an isolated spot of the West Texas desert where it will be left in the sand for your colleages to discover."

"Scott . . ." started Lasser.

"Not yet, Ross. You have to listen to a speech first," smiled Scott. Two I.T. Operationals entered the room and flanked Lasser.

"Gentlemen, here is an update on what is and is not happening."

"Lasser, you snot nose son of a bitch," growled Slade.

"Ross. Why?" asked Chase.

"That's immaterial, Chandler. Whether for power, money, ego satisfaction, control, conspiracy, or just another game to win, it doesn't now matter," noted Scott. "The fact is that our friend Ross has sold out. Apparently after our successes in Libya and Athens, some career types in the CIA, KGB, MI5, and the Mossad decided that they had better get their hands on me in an effort to neutralize I.T. One of their members already had Ross here reporting on what we were doing, and planning to do. They did this apparently freelance, which is all the more extraordinary. It seems most of the governments who have been bearing the burden of the results of terrorism, don't really mind our doing what they know they cannot do. But some of the career types are both professionally embarrassed and concerned about us as a potential threat to their activities. According to our reports, they intended—with the help of Mr. Lasser—to kidnap me, kill all of you, and make it appear that I had orchestrated a bloody coup. You would all have been heralded as righteous heroes cruelly misued by the xenomaniac Ingalls. Did you know, Ross, that you too were to die in their raid?''

''Serve the fucker right,'' sneered Danforth.

''What are you going to do?'' Lasser asked. Beads of sweat were pouring off his face, despite the room being airconditioned, and he felt incredibly nauseous.

''At first, the consensus was to kill you. But that is really too good for you pal. So we will send you back to your home. However, first you will be castrated and receive a free frontal lobotomy. Someday you may die in your own drool, but it won't be from our hands. You are the most contemptable scum imaginable, shitface. No more deals for you, pal. No more power. No more money, women, jets. When Doc Snyder gets through with you—no more fucking. I sentence you to life, asshole. Life as a vegetable, free to rot at your own pace.''

''Scott, please. Kill me instead,'' moaned Lasser.

''You've been dead for years, Ross. I can't kill you again.''

Everyone in the room stared at Lasser as he started to

sob uncontrollably. No longer the unbridled arrogance of wealth, power and youth—just fear, and an inimitable feeling of impending, inevitable loss.

"Take that pile of shit out of here," barked Morse.

"Scott? How did you find out?" asked Danforth.

"Trade secret, Remy. Suffice it to say, it's handled. After the unholy alliance lands in the desert with their hit team to find nothing but sidewinders and Gila monsters, they'll probably back off for a while. Meanwhile we need to do a few more things."

"Christ, we're screwed now. We'll never get any more support from the Board. Besides, you couldn't trust half those clowns," said Slade.

"Oh, we'll get support; and, we won't have to trust them. They are going to have to trust us," said Scott.

"No doubt you have another plan. Do you care to share it with us?" asked Moore.

"Public opinion is on our side right now. Senator Pastor said even the President doesn't really object to our work. We are going to do a little PR to compliment our operational arm," Scott began.

"This should be rich,'" laughed Slade. It was the first spark of humor injected in the room since everyone awoke.

"I am making another announcement to the world press tomorrow," stated Scott.

"You're turning into a regular media star. Iacocca, watch out," said Chase.

"Here's what I will say, and what I need you men to do for us." Scott proceeded to outline his speech and share his plan for positioning I.T.

CHAPTER FIFTY

The DC 10 flew over West Texas at 40,000 feet. Thirty-five thousand feet below, two helicopters loaded with the strike force mirrored the same course. Four Cobra attack helicopters flanked the formation. Garfield's heart rose to his epiglottis as the lead chopper reported what they sighted on the ground. Spelled out in the sand in large luminous letters was the message:

I.T. WELCOMES THE UNHOLY ALLIANCE OF THE CIA, KGB, MI5 AND MOSSAD TO THE PEACE AND EMPTINESS OF WEST TEXAS. Y'ALL HAVE A NICE DAY!

"I told you they were GOOD," said Wolf.

"Sorry about that, Brent," said Rosenburg.

"Where should we send the flowers, Mr. Garfield," said Gorky with a thin smile.

"Mr. Garfield?" It was the Captain of the DC 10 who had walked back to the cabin.

"Y-y-e-e-s?" he responded quietly.

"Mr. Garfield, I have been instructed to inform you that you have been relieved and that Mr. Gorky shall assume command. I have been ordered to land at Pensacola where we will be met."

"Yes, yes, of course," he responded. He arose and walked to the lavatory.

"Mr. Garfield?" the pilot called after him.

"Leave him alone. He's not going anywhere," said Rosenburg.

Thirty seconds later there was a gun shot and they all rushed back to the lavatory door, which was unlocked. They found Brent Garfield sitting on the commode with the top of his head missing and blood and brains running down the curved ceiling wall.

"Well at least he did the honorable thing," smiled Gorky.

"Hey, Jack, that could have been any one of us. If Ingalls had chosen Europe for his meeting, that could be you or me," growled Wolf.

"Well, what next?" asked Rosenburg.

"I say we leave I.T. to themselves. They can obviously do a better job than we can," said Wolf.

"That would be entirely unsatisfactory," retorted Gorky.

"Sure, since you clowns subsidize most of the terrorist assholes anyway," shouted Rosenburg.

"Gentlemen, the next step is totally out of our hands. What we are going to do is report back to our bosses, and they will tell us what to do or not to do," said Wolf quietly.

CHAPTER FIFTY-ONE

Scott was standing on the rim of the Grand Canyon. He wore a white two piece suit with a light blue shirt with thin white stripes and a white collar. He wore a dark blue necktie tied in a Windsor knot. He spoke into the camera after glancing at his notes once.

"Ladies and gentlemen, my name is Scott Ingalls. I am President of INTERNATIONAL TERRORIST SUPPRESSORS. A very great deal has happened since I spoke to you last. Some people are calling us saints, others sinners. In truth, we may be a little bit of each. When I last spoke to you, I stated our commitment to attack world-wide terrorism. That commitment holds firm. If we need to fill this canyon with the blood of terrorists, we shall. However, we intend to do much more than just serve as exterminators and garbage collectors. The scope of the good we can do is far greater.

"When we destroyed the Libyan terrorist training camp, we took something with us besides records and documents. We also captured about seven tons of gold bullion which apparently was being stored there to fund further terrorist activity. Fourteen thousand pounds of gold computes to a tad less than 180 million dollars U.S. Originally, we intended to use that money to fund our activities, since we had apparently lost much of our initial funding base. Many of those who attended the Geneva seminar, claim I bilked them out of the money they provided. Perhaps I did. However, now that we know what we can do, and how potentially effective we can be, I suggest that their money was well spent.

"Recently, members of a syndicate comprised of the CIA, KGB, MI5 and the Mossad attempted, on two separate occasions, to capture or kill me. They failed. Obviously.

"I am here today to suggest that I.T. can, and should be allowed to be effective in attacking terrorism.

"As a businessman, I realize you have to give a little to get a little. Therefore, here is what we are doing: the gold we confiscated from the terrorists is being delivered to two locations. Half is going to the Ethiopian relief effort; and, half to the city of Mexico City to help with rebuilding in the wake of the recent recurring earthquake crisis

"I.T. shall continue to be a benefactor to world-wide needs. In order to guarantee that we have the funds necessary to conduct our operations, and also engage in our philanthropy, we are herewith assessing a tax on international business. Each member of the original Board of Directors assembled in Geneva will remit, on a quarterly basis, one percent of their gross earnings to INTERNATIONAL TERRORIST SUPPRESSORS. Once a year, we will publish an annual report delineating how the money was utilized. Additionally, we are appealing to the private sector. Anyone in the free world may send a contribution to I.T., care of this address in Munich." The address was flashed on superimposed over the picture.

"To those of you who support our efforts, we humbly thank you for your support. To those who participated in the first Geneva meeting, this is not a request, but a mandate. World-wide business is hereby required to support the efforts of I.T. Failure to comply with this assessment shall be dealt with vigorously as only we know how to exercise vigor.

"Some will call this extortion. Some will consider it a small price to pay for unshackling an avenging archangel. Already, the PLO has agreed to confine their activities to Israeli military targets. Likewise, Israel has agreed to attack only confirmed terrorist targets. Elements of the IRA are meeting to determine how best to continue their struggle without suffering our wrath. The Red Brigade is reportedly 'talking.' We applaud these early signs of results. Nothing would please us more than to see the need for I.T. to be totally eliminated in the not too distant future.

"Eventually someone, or some agency may be successful in killing me. Should that happen, I.T. will continue. I am not I.T. I am merely the Chief Executive Officer. I can as easily be replaced as any lone infantryman. I.T. is a reality, ladies and gentlemen. I.T. is here—there—and everywhere it is needed. And, it shall continue to dole out our own brand of justice. When last I spoke to you I said that terrorism was a dishonorable activity, and that we would provide death for dishonor by violence of action. Our solution of extreme prejudice to terrorists shall become a constant. Terrorists everywhere, and anywhere should heed this message. Terrorism is no longer an acceptable solution or tactic. Terrorists, beware.

"Again, I ask for your moral and philosophical support. For those of you who can, and choose to do so, I ask your financial support.

"One final word to the bad guys. President Reagan once told you 'you can run, but you can't hide.' Remember, I.T. is every bit as committed. Except we are not shackled with the moral, ethical, or political constraints Mr. Reagan was forced to suffer. We won't give you time to run. If we come after you—and we WILL—we promise you a jihad. We will kill not only terrorists, but their entire families. We will burn their villages and desecrate their temples. We hold the markers on your karma—you need not wait for your next reincarnation to pay debts owed. There are only two options now available to those who practice terrorism: meet my promise, or a swift suicide.'' The screen faded to white.

CHAPTER FIFTY-TWO

The dessert dishes of devoured zabaglione were being removed by a busboy as a waiter wheeled up a cart with brandies and cigars.

"Two Monte Cruz, two Remy Martins, and—Jen?" asked Scott.

"Drambuie, please." She smiled.

"Well, Scott—what now. Unlike the monkey with his fist in the jar, you don't have the option of just opening your hand to get free. Despite this recent apparent covert cooperation from the government, you are now not only a target for any terrorist group in the world, but a most well publicized target," said Calvin.

"But he's better looking than Iacocca," grinned Jennifer.

"And far better protected, believe me," said Scott.

"Come on, Scott. What are you going to do? Your recent exploits seem to have slowed down terrorist activity—as if they really believe your threats about killing parents, women and children—"

"Cal. . . . I realize this may sound awful, but I do. Forgive me, Jen, but we truly believe that the death of the family of a terrorist is well worth it if it can impede the use of terrorism as an acceptable, or even laudable tactic."

Calvin drew on his cigar and looked from his wife to his friend. He dropped his eyes to the ashtray and flicked an ash. "They'll kill you, you know?"

"Yes. Eventually, they probably will. The two key questions are which 'They,' and when? Look, guy, I.T. is my brainchild. I planned it; founded it; and, more or less direct it. But I am not it. Now that the mechanism exists it has developed its own synergy. I.T. will continue with or without me. It is my legacy to a troubled and frequently fucked up world. Let history judge me Cal."

"I need to hit the head. Is my wife safe here with the infamous Scott Ingalls?" asked Calvin.

"Safer than safe," Scott answered.

Calvin got up from the table and dropped his napkin on his chair. He picked up his cigar and headed for the men's room.

"How bad is it, Scott?" asked Jennifer.

"Not that bad—nowhere near normal—but not all that bad. I've got money, comrades, colleagues, occasionally the company of a good woman I happen to love—and I've lost a few friends."

"Not this one."

"Thanks for that. It means a lot. I'm really sorry about Cal."

"Don't confuse the form with the substance. He takes his job and it's responsibilities very seriously. His biggest problem with you is he respects you, and although he will never admit it, I think he might even be a little proud of what you have done—if not how you've done it."

"He really feels I betrayed our friendship?"

"He says that—mostly I think as an excuse. You know Cal, right is right and wrong is wrong. Black and white—he has difficulties with the gray scale. Lord knows, you have never been black or white."

"For whatever it's worth, Jen, I'll help him however I can—even though I realize he can never help me."

"Never say never, Mr. Ingalls. Maggie Rice said you could never fall in love."

"Fuck Maggie Rice."

"Yes, I heard you did." She smiled.

Calvin returned from the men's room without his cigar and looking refreshed.

"Well, Jen . . . did you convince Genghis Khan here to give himself up to the World Court at the Hague? By the way, the meanest looking rock-like black man is in the men's room. He never said a word—just kinda half smiled? Is he one of yours?"

"Rucker tends toward the stoic. A real pussycat."

"Looked more like a panther on steroids," scowled Calvin.

"You wouldn't believe half of what's true about the man, but believe me, no drugs have ever passed those lips—except for beer, and then only in appropriate moderation."

"I'm sure he's a wonderful human being and a credit to his race. But I don't care about him. I do care about you—or at least I did once."

"Cal, I appreciate that and I most sincerely regret any problems I may have caused for you by our past association. Things will work out. And although you may find it hard to accept right now, eventually, we will be able to help each other," said Scott.

"Scotty, you may be beyond any help. However, the good Lord helps those who help themselves. I may be able to salvage my political ass, but I can't see anyway I can ever help you—given the direction you have chosen," sighed Cal.

"Time will tell, Senator. In the meantime, I promised you an explanation as to what the spark was that ignited my crusade. Despite your rhetoric about vigilantism and misguided terrorism on my part, I do feel I owe you that explanation, although no other living soul, including Colonel Morse and Leslie Campbell, know, what I'm about to tell you.'' Scott took a cigar out of his leather cigar case and cut the end off. He picked up a book of matches and after a brief gesture to Jennifer suggesting a request for approval to light up, he lighted the cigar.

''Cal, everything I have told you is true. I've already beat it to death, so I won't rehash the basic pitch. The one catalyst which no one knows is both very private and very very secret. It is no big secret however that after I got out of the Army and before I hit New York, I did some freelance work for the Company—the CIA. Most of that work was related to Southeast Asia since that was my area of expertise. However, I was involved in one project which included a diamond smuggling group out of Johanassburg. While reviewing those files, I discovered something which at first didn't sink in—but ten years later, it did.''

''And that was the mysterious spark that ignited I.T.?'' asked Jennifer.

''Yes. In a way you could say that. Anyway, to make a long story short, a small piece of data I discovered in 1976 sent off bells and whistles in 1988. I was doing research for a client involved in bauxite export for a large Aluminum conglomerate,'' said Scott.

''You're starting to lose me, pal,'' said Cal.

''I'm already lost,'' sighed Jennifer.

''Okay, here's the capsule. The plane in which my parents were killed was not involved in a simple accident as reported. There was no pilot error involved. A Black terrorist group seeking a showpiece cornerstone for their propoganda blew up that plane—and my parents.'' Scott paused to flick an ash.

"How come it never came out?" asked Cal.

"Ah, well, apparently it wasn't 'appropriate' at the time. The CIA crashed in before any claims could be made. They neutralized the entire operation. All the bad guys (there were less than fifty) were killed. It was arranged that the airline would receive considerable government concessions and supplemental contracts if they cooperated in proving the crash was mechanical and or pilot error as was eventually reported."

"Oh, Scott, I'm so sorry for you," said Jennifer.

"But there is no question about it, my friends. My parents—two of the most loving, giving, apolitical people ever to grace this planet were killed—murdered—in a covered up terrorist attack which killed over 200 innocent passengers and crew." Scott reached for his brandy and stared vacant eyed at the tip of his cigar.

"Why didn't you tell me this on that fishing trip?" asked Calvin.

"Several reasons. Not the least of which is why you two can never repeat the story—not that anyone would believe you anyway," said Scott.

"And that is?" asked Cal.

"Senator, whether you like it or not, I.T. is viable. We have proved that. The results speak for themselves. You said it yourself, even the President thinks we can do some good. That's one reason I'm here in Newport speaking in Top Secret sessions with various Pentagon big shots at the War College."

"So your big stick theory works. What harm is there in humanizing your crusade? It might even help you add to your groundswell of popular support," asked Cal.

"Cal, I have 'what if-ed' this to death. It is imperative to our continued success that no one ever know, or even presume, that Scott Ingalls is anything but a maurauding xenomaniac. No one must ever think that I am, behind the head wielding threats and promises of genocide, a sensitive, hurt child attempting to prevent future children from suffering the loss of their parents to a game they have no part in.''

There was a long moment of silence during which no one chose to make eye contact with anything except their drink glasses on the table.

Colonel Morse appeared at the top of the stairs and gestured to Scott.

''Time's up, sport. We need to be in the wind,'' said Morse.

Cal looked over to Morse and turned to Scott. ''So, there's your living legend? Big one, isn't he, Jen?''

''Quite impressive. Do they all look like that, Scott?'' asked Jennifer.

''No, they don't. But they all share elements of his essence. I'm sorry, I have to leave. I've enjoyed this dinner, and I can only hope it has in some way helped to explain some of what I must do. Remember, what I have shared with you two is just between the three of us—forever and always. It must be.''

''We promise,'' said Jennifer.

''Oh, yeah. I realize you may not want him to have this, but here's an autographed picture of Uncle Scott for Steven. You can give it to him, or line your bird cage with it. You two take care. And Cal—for whatever it's worth—I'm betting on big things for you in the future. I hope I live to see you reach your full potential. Jen'd make a great looking First Lady.''

Scott left his two old friends to finish their drinks in private. When he and Morse got to the bottom of the stairs, the Colonel turned to him. "Well? Don't keep me in the dark. What did you tell them?" asked Morse.

Scott smiled and pulled on his raincoat. "I lied! Like a cheap rug. I made up a story sure to capture their hearts," said Scott.

"Ha-ha-ha. You prick. Come on, sport, let's get out of here. I've got Naval Intelligence thinking they've got you on the run halfway around Jamestown Island right now. We shook their tail, but I need to get you out of the States for a while. Word is a splinter group of the Red Brigade is planning another hit on NATO headquarters and the Unholy Alliance is reportedly regrouping for one last go at you," said Morse as they entered the parking lot.

"I've got an idea for pulling their fangs, Colonel. Have Jerry assemble the staff and I'll fill you in," said Scott.

The big dark blue Mercedes pulled out of the small parking lot and turned left onto the narrow one way street before turning left twice more. They passed by Hunter House and turned right onto the causeway out to Goat Island. When they came to the hotel's parking lot, the car turned left again and rolled down to the private dock. Xing and Bond were waiting on the dock as a forty-two-foot Invader sportsfisherman idled stern to, with its bow pointing out into the harbor.

As soon as Scott and Morse stepped aboard, the boat revved up and pulled away from the dock turning out of the harbor and out to sea.

To any observers it appeared like another rich boat owner going for a midnight ride—probably with some young female companion about to have her virtue compromised.

Scott accepted a hot cup of coffee and outlined his plan.

CHAPTER FIFTY-THREE

The Invader, with the name *Bad Penney* painted on the transom, had just cleared the Brenton Reef lightship when Scott finished briefing the I.T. Operational Detachment staff.

"I don't like it, sport," said Morse.

"I don't know, Colonel, it has its charm," smiled Jerry Kapstein.

"Charm, my military ass. What if those fuckers decide to just off our long haired buddy there?" Morse was looking through the notes taken during Scott's briefing.

"Then you get to revenge my early demise Colonel," said Scott.

Sidney Bullerwell loaded his pipe and added, "I agree with Jerry, sir. Yes, there is a risk. But if Mr. Ingalls here can't stall these blokes for the time needed, I'm a ballerina. He could bullshit a TV evangelist."

"Chung? What do you think?" asked Scott.

"We have had the opportunity to review the profiles of the remaining members of this 'Unholy Alliance.' I do not think they will kill you until they have spoken and heard you speak. Your timing will have to be precise. However, I believe you can do it. You are not faster than me, but these senior level government spies—you can do it," said Xing.

"Fuck! I still don't like it. Why not send me, or Xing, or even Jerry?" asked Morse.

"Because they probably would just kill you. No. It's me they want. I am the one they perceive has injured their professional pride. Arguments to the contrary, all indications are that this has turned 'personal' with them. Gorky would kill me on sight if he could. But the others—Wolf, and Rosenburg—they want to revenge Garfield, and tweak my nose." Scott smiled.

"You're letting your ego put your dick in a wringer, sport. What does this plan really accomplish?" asked Morse.

"Colonel, ego is a very small part of this plan. What it accomplishes is considerable. It gets the 'Unholy Alliance' off our ass, it puts them out of business—and it pays them back for Devens and Lasser," said Scott.

"Fucking-A!" chimed Kapstein.

"All right already," sighed Morse, "but we stack the deck—or we don't do it. If Mr. Ingalls is resigning his chair-borne status, he'll follow my fucking tactical plan."

"I wouldn't have it any other way, Colonel," smiled Scott.

"You know you can be a perfect asshole sometimes, Scott. I've half a mind to let those spooks have you," grunted Morse.

"Colonel, you just be there when I need you. Then you can spank me later," laughed Scott.

CHAPTER FIFTY-FOUR

The remains of the Unholy Alliance were seated in a small hotel room in Virginia Beach. Wolf and Rosenburg were clad casually in polo shirts and shorts. Gorky looked out of place in his light two piece gray suit with white shirt and club tie.

"What is the purpose of this meeting? I was under the impression our work regarding I.T. was concluded—and unsuccessful," said Gorky.

Wolf leaned forward and put a cassette in a tape recorder. "I received this telephone call at my home. On an unsecured open line," he snapped.

He turned on the machine and the three spies listened to the conversation.

"Mr. Rosenburg, my name is Scott Ingalls. I believe you know who I am?"

"Are you the fellow on those TV messages about some vigilante effort to kill terrorists?" asked Rosenburg's voice.

There was a short pause.

"Okay. Look, Rosenburg. You know who I am, and I know who you are. This is a one time only offer. As we speak a package is being delivered to your associate in London. Mr. Wolf will have all the details of what I propose. You talk to him, then get ahold of Gorky. I will meet with the three of you one time only—under the terms outlined in the package delivered to Wolf. If the three of you concur, you can have a face-to-face with me. If not, I will be like a single grain of sand in the Sahara for you to find. If you choose to kill me, I suggest you at least wait until we have spoken. David, the terms I have outlined are not negotiable, and they will not be presented twice.''

''I understand,'' said Rosenburg's voice.

''Be there or be square, pal. *L'Chaim!*''

The three intelligence officers exchanged looks and Wolf dropped a file on the coffee table.

''What means this 'be there or be square'?'' asked Gorky.

''It means we get one more chance, asshole,'' said Rosenburg.

''Why does he do this? He is too arrogant. Let us just kill him and be about our business,'' said Gorky.

''He does need killing, David—no questions about that,'' said Wolf.

''I'm torn,'' said Rosenburg. ''Why would he put himself at risk like this? His terms were rigid, but we could still obviously kill him. What do you think, Harrison?''

''I don't see the hook. He can't plan on killing us. He says he'll permit us to search him. He'll come unarmed. He insists on a helicopter which means he'll probably have us tracked and or escorted by air. I say we go ahead with the meet. I talked to my boss, and he agrees. We use our own pilot in their aircraft, and keep Mr. Ingalls with us so they can't shoot down the chopper,'' said Wolf.

"We should kill him," said Gorky.

"I hate to agree with you—but we probably should," said Rosenburg. "But first, I want to hear him out. The son of a bitch called me at home—on an open line."

"His intelligence is far too good. He obviously has identified us. What's to prevent him from targeting us for elimination?" asked Gorky.

"If he hasn't already," said Rosenburg.

"So it's agreed? We meet with him on his terms?" asked Wolf.

"Yes," said Rosenburg.

"And then we kill him," added Gorky.

". . . and then we kill him," said Wolf and Rosenburg in unison.

CHAPTER FIFTY-FIVE

"Ingalls, you thick headed son of a bitch," moaned Morse. "I just hope I'm not around the day your big ass luck decides to take a holiday."

"Colonel, today you are my luck—and all leaves are cancelled. You be there when I need you," said Scott.

"Like a guardian angel, sport. Jer, is everything else set?" asked the big man.

"Handled. Let's go throw this Christian into the lions' den," smiled Kapstein.

Gorky, Wolf and Rosenburg had picked up the helicopter at the designated spot and had a team spend an hour combing it over for bugs, booby traps and anything vaguely suspicious. When they were satisfied the chopper was sterile, they took off for the rendez-vous point. They were accompanied by a fixed wing aircraft flying some twenty thousand feet over head. The plan called for them to be on the ground only twenty seconds to permit Scott to board before flying off into the wilderness of the California High Sierras.

When the chopper set down on the LZ, Scott drove a motorcycle out to the aircraft, dropped it in the dirt by the skid, and boarded. As soon as he was on board the helicopter took off and headed northeast.

"Gentlemen. I believe you have been wanting to meet me. I am Scott Ingalls."

The three men stared at Scott and then Gorky stepped forward and commenced searching Scott. He expertly crushed the fabric of his jacket and trousers, shamelessly felt into his crotch and the crack of his ass, and ripped open his shirt. "He's clean," announced Gorkey.

"I would have unbuttoned the shirt, Ivan. You didn't need to rip the shirt,"' said Scott.

"And you didn't need to give Lasser a lobotomy," jibed Wolf.

"Oh, but we did. But we're not here to talk about past actions, are we?" asked Scott.

"Just what are we here for, Mr. Ingalls?" asked Rosenburg.

"Well, David, I believe you intend to kill me. Hopefully, after we have had an opportunity to talk."

"If you are so sure we intend to kill you, why did you come?" asked Wolf.

"Several reasons. First, of course, is professional curiosity. Second, albeit perhaps naive, to ask you not to kill me." Scott smiled.

"And what if we just kill you?" asked Gorky.

"Yes, as much as it pains me to agree with our card carrying colleague, the idea has certain merit," added Wolf.

"Ah—if you summarily killed me right now, you wouldn't have the opportunity to find out how I knew who you were, what David's private unlisted phone number is, what post office box Harrison uses for private correspondence, or why Ivan continues sexual liaisons with both a male and female dancer from the Bolshoi."

"He lies—kill him," shouted Gorky.

"No!" interrupted Rosenburg. "He neither lies, nor dies—not just yet anyway. You are a remarkable man, Mr. Ingalls. Just what else do you know, or think you know?"

"At last—to the cobb. Very well. If you can keep your AC/DC comrade from wasting me a few minutes longer, I'll share what I know, in the hope you will do likewise before making a martyr of me," said Scott.

"Martyrs never get to appreciate their martyrdom," said Wolf.

"You three men, and the late Brent Garfield of the CIA, were ordered by your immediate superiors to infiltrate and learn all you could about my organization. You started with Lasser who had been in bed with the Mossad since his college days. His mother and sister were victims of Auschwitz, and his father, who survived became a rabid freelancer for the Mossad. Through him you learned about me, I.T., and our little mercenary army. Somehow, and I admit, we aren't quite sure how, you switched a young Montana cowboy named Devens with one of your agents . . ."

". . . a target of opportunity. We had been grooming our man for years until a need arrived. You just created the need for the available tool," said Gorky.

". . . anyway, we killed your substitute, and proceeded with our plan to destroy the Libyan camp. Tell me, David, Harrison, did you know Ivan's team had that new VX gas, and biological agents targeted for England, Israel, and Brasil, as well as the United States?"

"There were no such agents—another futile effort at disinformation by your amateurs," scowled Gorky.

Wolf held up an interrupting hand.

"Oh, they were there—I reviewed the data I.T sent to the press. You did us a favor with that, Scott—no question—but that favor doesn't overshadow the potential threat your group poses to our other operations," said Wolf.

"Enough of this—let's just shoot him and be done with this charade," said Gorky.

"Shoot me—stab me—or throw me out of the chopper, it won't alter your fate. You clowns are through," said Scott.

"For a man in your position, your arrogance is out of place. Do you really harbor any hope of surviving this meeting?" asked Wolf.

"It depends. I figure Ivan here may take a fancy to me. I'm told I have adorable, tight buns. He likes tight buns. He may either try to kiss me or throw my butt out the door."

Gorky screamed a string of Russian obscenities and shoved Scott out the door of the helicopter. "No-o-o-o-o . . ." Rosenburg tried to stop Gorky but was too late. Scott was falling from 10,000 feet toward the ground.

"Why did you try to stop me, you Zionist Jew bastard?" cried Gorky.

"Because he wanted you to push him out, you fool," said Rosenburg.

"But what did he accomplish by that?" asked Wolf.

At the moment Scott was pushed from the chopper a sidewinder missile was fired from the I.T. aircraft which was tracking the Alliance escort plane and the chopper. The Alliance aircraft erupted in a ball of flame just as the pilot identified the incoming missile. The three remaining members of the Unholy Alliance heard the explosion and looked out to the falling Ingalls as comprehension dawned on their faces and drained all color.

CHAPTER FIFTY-SIX

Morse, Kapstein and Xing had been monitoring Scott's conversation with the Unholy Alliance from the transmitter which was sewn into his leather suspenders. When they heard Gorky's rage toward Scott, two things happened at once. First, Xing ordered the missile fired at the escort plane. At the same time, Morse and Kapstein jumped out of the back of the plane. They were already freefalling toward the helicopter when Scott was pushed from the door.

Scott went into a full spread eagle to reduce his fall as much as possible. Morse and Kapstein went into deltas to speed up their falls toward Scott. As they neared his position in the air they slowed down and moved in toward Ingalls.

Jerry handed a parachute to Scott, and he and Morse helped the I.T. President fasten it on. Scott was all hooked up with the altimeter on Morse's reserve chute showed 2,000 feet. He tapped Scott on the shoulder and moved away as all three men deployed their parachutes. The parasails they had on gently carried them to the field where they all three executed stand up landings. They pulled off the chutes and started to laugh.

"Fucking-a-bob," shouted Morse. We not only got the whole thing on tape . . ."

"Sid had the entire transmission simulcast to CIA, MI6, KGB, and the Mossad," smiled Jerry.

"Yup! I think it safe to assume your basic 'Unholy Fucking-Alliance' is shit out of business," laughed Morse.

"See, Colonel. Oh, ye of little faith," said Scott.

"Hey! It worked. Okay, already. That doesn't alter the fact it was a damn risky and stupid thing to try," said Morse.

"Boss—you said it all already—it worked," said Kapstein.

Their repartee was interrupted by the sound of a helicopter approaching over the trees.

"There's Chacon. Let's book. We still need to link up with the guys in Europe before the Red Brigade takes out the entire NATO staff," said Scott.

"Why hurry? That's Walter Buckley's command, and I never did like that arrogant son of a bitch," said Morse.

Kapstein looked at Morse and then Scott.

"Aw shit. I'm kidding, guys. Actually, it will piss him off more if we save his ass than if we let him fry," smiled Morse.

Scott smiled and slapped Morse on the shoulder. "Well then by all means. Let's go piss off General Buckley."

Don't forget nothing.

Have your musket clean as a whistle, hatchet scoured, sixty rounds powder and ball and be ready to march at a minute's warning.

When you're on the march, act the way you would if you was sneaking up on a deer. See the enemy first.

Tell the truth about what you see and what you do. There is an army depending on us for correct information. You can lie all you please when you tell other folks about the Rangers, but don't ever lie to a Ranger or Officer.

Don't never take a chance you don't have to.

When we're on the march, we march single file, far enough apart so one shot can't go through two men.

If we strike swamps, or soft ground, we spread out abreast, so it's hard to track us.

When we march, we keep moving till dark, so as to give the enemy the least possible chance at us.

When we camp, half the party stays awake while the other half sleeps.

If we take prisoners, we keep 'em separate till we have had time to examine them, so they can't cook up a story between 'em.

Don't ever march home the same way. Take a different route so you won't be ambushed.

No matter whether we travel in big parties or little ones, each party has to keep a scout twenty yards ahead, twenty yards on each flank and twenty yards in the rear, so the main body can't be surprised and wiped out.

Every night you'll be told where to meet if surrounded by a superior force.

Don't sit down to eat without posting sentries.

Don't sleep beyond dawn. Dawn's when the French and Indians attack.

Don't cross a river by a regular ford.

If somebody's trailing you, make a circle, come

back onto your own tracks, and ambush the folks that aim to ambush you.

Don't stand up when the enemy's coming against you. Kneel down, lie down, hide behind a tree.

Let the enemy come till he's almost close enough to touch. Then let him have it and jump out and finish him up with your hatchet.

—Standing order, Rogers' Rangers,
Major Robert Rogers 1756

ACKNOWLEDGEMENTS

I had always considered Acknowledgments in novels to be gratuitous verbiage performed as a courtesy and designed by Publishers to present an author's false modesty, and add to the page count. Now that I have to write this, I realize my former impressions were myopic.

In anything which takes sixteen years to finish there are a great many people who contribute, both directly and indirectly. I first came up with the concept for I.T. while laying in traction in Martin Army Hospital at Fort Benning, Georgia. Six years later I added to the concept based on changes in my life. During the summer of 1985 in the wake of wifely "urging," I finally sat down and finished the manuscript you now hold.

Scott Ingalls is a synthesis of fact and fiction. He and I share much in common. However, he is a prime example of an author's license to improve upon reality. The primary difference between Scott Ingalls and Geoffrey Metcalf, is that Scott does what I would have liked to do but lacked the courage to undertake. The frightening thing is that I really believe the basic concept and organization of I.T. could work, but would take better men than this writer to effect it.

In acknowledging who contributed to this novel there is

a long list of those who by influence, support or impression contributed. First and last my bride, Linda, was without question the catalyst. She caused me to finish a task which had become an exercise in procrastination. My parents, Ted and Gloria, provided me with much, far beyond life. Much of the sophistication, and attitudinal positioning I now have is a direct result of opportunities provided by two loving, giving parents. My brother Greg (one of the best Charter Boat Captains in Rhode Island). John Cerra, my high school wrestling coach, who had a profound effect on my early development and made Airborne school seem almost like a cakewalk. Anyone who survived a Saturday practice with "the old man" could coast through what for many at Benning is considered a nightmare. There is a list of nameless faces I shared time and pain with in Ranger school, but Captain Christianson, SFC Magwood and SFC Burnell remain distinct. The National Guard students I instructed in the OCS and NCO programs of the Rhode Island Military Academy. The Officers and men of the 19th and 20th Special Forces Group I served with in Company D and Company C. The Officers and NCO's I commanded in the 115th Military Police Company. Friends and foes in the 118th Military Police Battalion and 43d Military Police Brigade, especially my former battalion commander Joe DelSesto (who makes a cameo appearance here). The Late LTC "Bull" Simmons and the entire group of Son Tay raiders. Ross Perot for what he did for his men in Iran proving that the private sector is capable of doing what governments cannot.

Special friends who remained so through the good and bad: Larry McCracken, that special breed of friend who provides help without making you ask, and does so with grace and affection; my hunting and fishing partners Tom

Pate and Stevie DiGioia; my favorite Queen Bee, Connie Hall; and another author who fights the same fight, Janet Taber.

Wordprocessing—without which frustration with my fast but inconsistent typing skills would have driven this story back into a box. Darby, my faithful and thickheaded yellow lab who sat with me throughout the grueling hours of write and rewrite deserves some credit for which I will take him duck hunting every year the rest of his life.

There is a long list of others I won't bore you with, but who remain in my thoughts and affection.

Special thanks to the folks at Critic's Choice, especially Ann Kearns whose criticism of the original manuscript hopefully resulted in a better final book.

Last, as first, is Linda, who provided me with love, affection, sympathy, ass kickings, support (both moral and material), and the inimitable pride and joy of being her best friend and husband.

Geoffrey M. Metcalf
Sacramento, California
October 1987